The
Black Boy's
Artistic Odyssey

A Tale of Art, Dreams, and Triumph

Tebogo Khalo

TEBOGO KHALO

The Black Boy's Artistic Odyssey

A Tale of Art, Dreams, and Triumph.

First published by Thoughts Keepers 2024

Printed in South Africa

Cover Design by Tebogo Khalo with DALL.E

Edited by Thabang Khalo and Andisa Gcaba

For permissions, please contact:

hello@tebogokhalo.com

www.tebogokhalo.com

First edition

ISBN: 978-0-7961-9891-4

This book was professionally typeset on Reedsy.
Find out more at reedsy.com

This book is dedicated to my younger self. I hope he is happy and proud of us.

Contents

Acknowledgments

First and foremost, I would want to offer my heartfelt gratitude, honour, and love where it is due. This book would not have been possible without the help and encouragement of many amazing people who have been by my side throughout this journey. Who better to start with than my mother, Kenosi Khalo, the most beautiful, kind-hearted, loving, and cheerful lady on the planet! Mom, I know you're not much of a reader, but one thing is certain: you're my biggest supporter. So you'll probably be reading this section of the book just to show your love, support, and keenness in what I do. I write to you because you have been such an important part of my life, and this is my way of saying thank you. You are everything to me: my universe, my light, and my warrior. Mama, I love you so much. I will continue to make you proud, and one day I will fulfill all of your wishes and build you your ideal home. To my brother, who has always been there for and beside me. My soldier, guide, and pillar of strength. Even though things were not always easy growing up, I am glad and pleased to have you as a brother. You've always taught me to look at life with a more hopeful outlook. I enjoy the enthusiasm and positivity you bring into my life. You often say I inspire you, yet you are the one who inspires me with your diligent and consistent attitude. You have always been my role model and someone I look up to. I'd like to thank you for being a part of my novel, for inspiring my characters, and for being an honest, critical, and caring beta reader who provided constructive and outstanding positive comments. I love you, Thabang Khalo.

Anna Kganyane, I cannot thank you enough. You've been both a father and aunt—a genuine matriarch. You are kind-hearted, enjoyable to be around, curious about life, and extremely knowl-edgeable. I always look forward to visiting your home because the environment is filled with love and a welcome vibe. Most significantly, I appreciate your financial teachings. Thank you for teaching us about money and assisting us financially. I am very appreciative of your continued emotional and financial support. Aunt Anna, I love you. I am grateful to the Ramela family for their unwavering support and affection for my family and me. Thank you, Lebogang Ramela, for your kindness and support during my time at university. Freddie Ramela, I appreciate your kindness and grace, as well as the financial insights you've shared with me. Atang Ramela, my dear brother, your humility and kindness are inspirational. I truly admire the zeal and courage you possess, young man. Continue to embrace these qualities, as they define you. I hold deep respect and affection for you and am proud of the person you are. Naledi Ramela, you are the sister I have always dreamed of. Your advice, insightful words, and constructive criticism have been a godsend in helping me become a better person. Kwanda Lamour Ramela, I appreciate that we have a common vision. Thank you for being such an inspiring fellow. Thank you, Ramela family, for all you've done and continue to do. I love you all a lot.

Mamani and Rangwane, my wonderful grandparents, I cannot thank you enough for everything you've done for me, my brother, and my mother. Without your love and support, we would not be who we are today. You taught us the value of family, the power of education, and how to love and share love. Growing up under your care has been the most wonderful blessing. You inspired the creativity of a dreamer in me and showed me there is a better world out there. We will carry on your legacy by teaching the next generation about a world full of love, hope, faith, and joy. Thank you for all of the teachings and hope you have given me; they have saved my life. Honour to the Moswetsa Family. Thank you, Sebolelo Moswetsa, for being someone I can trust. You have saved me from myself in ways that you cannot comprehend. Your genuine compassion, faith, and open-heartedness have helped me stay grounded in God. Thank you for your tenderness and sensible remarks at times of trouble. I am sincerely appreciative. Thank you, John Moswetsa, for assisting my mother with her spiritual journey in Christ. Thank you, Bothlale Moswetsa, for understanding and always making me feel capable. I hope I have taught you good lessons in return. I adore you all, Moswetsa family.

Litau Noge, you're a great father. Even when I loathed you as a child, and everyone in the family disapproved of you, you stayed. You persevered. Despite the vitriol directed at you, you continued to love Mom and shared that love with me and my brother. Today, I am a man who understands what it is to love, how to love a woman, how to be kind to her, and how to fight for love. I've learned to appreciate your peculiarities while focusing on the positive you've given to our family. You have taken better care of my uncle, Badirwand Reginald Mapodi Rapulane, than anybody else. I'm really appreciative of what you've done. I love you, Litau Noge. Thank you so much, and may peace always be with you. Andisa Gcaba, words cannot express the delight and thankfulness I feel when I write about you, my love. Thank you for being such an important part of my book and my biggest fan. I am really glad to have you at my side throughout this journey.

From the very beginning, you have shown immense support for my dream of writing a book. Your optimistic interest in my ideas pushed me to take the leap and start writing, turning a long-held dream into reality. You have been involved in every level of this process, from the basic concept to the final editing. Your diligent attention to detail and candid feedback have proven beneficial. You assisted me with the editing, were a continual source of support and encouragement, and even provided your voice for the audiobook. Your trust in me and the project has kept me motivated and inspired. I trust your input and appreciate your critical insight and honesty, which have greatly enhanced this work. Thank you for supporting me through the highs and lows, the beautiful and tough times. Your love and support made all the difference. Andisa Nobuhle Gcaba, I really love you. Here's to many more years of growing together in love.

Giving thanks to the Rapulane Family, Dorothy Rapuane, I am profoundly thankful for the love and joy you have brought to my life. Having you as my grandma is a tremendous blessing, and I want to thank you for the important role you play in my life. Your knowledge, caring presence, and great cuisine have provided comfort and nourishment in many different of ways. Thank you for supporting me emotionally, spiritually, psychologically, and physically. Your comforting love and advice have fashioned me into the person I am today, and I am very grateful for everything you have done. Your presence is a treasured gift, and I am deeply appreciative for the insight and care you offer. Thank you, Mpho Rapulane, for being such an awesome sister. Your unfailing support has been the foundation of my existence. Your insightful remarks, teachings, and cautions have helped me overcome numerous obstacles and added enormous value to my path. Your love and encouragement have been an unwavering source of strength, and I will be eternally thankful for everything you've done for me. I love you, and I treasure our relationship dearly. Lebohang Rapulane, your stern love, kindness, and encouragement have been essential to me. You've always been there with a consoling word and a listening ear, offering advice and knowledge that helped shape my path. Your advice and caution have helped me negotiate life's challenges with greater clarity and confidence. Thank you for being a wonderful sister. I love you and am incredibly grateful for your presence in my life. Kamogelo Lenake, you have a unique place in my heart. Your love, encouragement, and inspiration have been a source of light in my life. The enjoyable times we've had together, as well as the encouragement you've given me, have meant everything to me. Your presence has always provided comfort and delight. Thank you for being such a wonderful brother to me and for the many ways you have enriched my life. I appreciate you more than words can say. Thank you very much.

Kagiso Rapulane (Cage the Aesthetic), growing up next to you has been a huge blessing. I've always been fascinated by your creative abilities and aesthetic sense. The love, encouragement, and enjoyable experiences we've had have enhanced my life in so many ways. Your ability to recognise beauty in the world and express it artistically has been an ongoing source of inspiration. Thank you for being such a wonderful brother and bringing so much joy into my life. I am really grateful for you. Kgomotso Segole, even though we don't communicate as frequently as we used to, I want you to know how important you are to me. Your companionship has always brought me strength and joy. The moments we had, full of laughter and profound talks, have had a lasting influence. Our friendship spans space and time, and I treasure every moment we've made together. I love you and respect our relationship very much. Simphiwe Maduna, your unrelenting dedication and genuine spirit have always stuck out to me. Even though we don't communicate very often, your friendship has been a continual source of comfort and inspiration. Our days together were memorable, and I will always remember them. Your presence in my life is a blessing, and I value our relationship very much. I love you and am thankful for the relationship we share. Blessing Raditsele, your name accurately describes the influence you have had on my life. Despite our few chats, your generosity and warmth have always been a source of light. Over the years, you've provided me with essential support and understanding. Our friendship is a gift that I cherish, no matter how many miles or months separate us. I value our relationship and love you very much. Teboho Malape, your contagious excitement and bright attitude on life have always inspired me. Although our discussions are few and far between, your friendship continues to have a tremendous influence on me. The recollections of our time together put a smile on my face and warmth in my heart. Our friendship demonstrates that real ties do not fade with time or distance. I value you and our relationship more than words can say. I love you so much. I'd want to express my heartfelt appreciation to Lindiwe Radebe, an amazing friend of my mother, whose support has helped bring this book to reality. Your kind financial contributions enabled me to complete this project, for which I am very grateful. Your confidence in my work and encouragement have meant more to me than words can say. Thank you for being an important part of this journey. Nhlanhla Gamede, our friendship has grown stronger over the years, from high school to university. You continue to be my strength throughout university life, and your unfailing encouragement and contagious humour made even the most difficult days tolerable. Your determination and tenacity have been an ongoing source of inspiration for me. Your strength and positivism showed through as we faced the trials and successes of university life together. I am immensely proud of what you have accomplished and thrilled to see what the future holds for you. Continue to shine and motivate the people around you. I admire and value you more than words can explain. Thabo Tumane, from the lively conversations and debates of high school to the bright experiences of university, your inexhaustible energy and love for life added so much delight to my path. Whether we were arguing the newest political topic or simply hanging out, your knowledge and enthusiasm made an indelible effect. You've continually proven the value of sticking to one's principles and aiming for greatness. Your constant passion and enthusiasm have been a source of inspiration. I am really pleased with your successes and believe you will continue making waves. Thank you for being a continual source of inspiration and bringing so much life to our shared experiences. I greatly respect and admire you. Refilwe Ntsooa, from a helpful buddy in high school to a sensitive confidant at university, your generosity and sensitivity have deeply impacted my heart. You were always available to listen and soothe me, providing support and understanding when I needed it the most. Our meaningful chats and shared experiences have had an everlasting impact on my life. Your ability to provide compassion and insight has helped me overcome several problems. I am extremely proud of the kind and determined individual you have become. Continue to pursue your desires and dreams with the same grace and passion you've always had. Your friendship means everything to me, and I admire and appreciate you much.

Hlawutelo Msisinyani and Sizwe Zwane, your presence has brought so much colour to my university experience. Your relentless commitment and sense of humour made every day at university a beautiful experience. You had a knack for making everyone around you feel appreciated and involved, which is an uncommon talent. The memories we made, from late-night laughter to youthful, wild, and free-living, will always have a special place in my heart. The memories we had together will be treasured forever, and while life pulls us in separate directions, let us never forget the fantastic times we had. I am extremely proud of your development and accomplishments, and I am confident that you will continue to excel. Thank you for being such great friends. Continue to achieve great success in life. I deeply respect and admire you.

I owe a debt of gratitude to several authors whose works have profoundly influenced my own writing journey:

Thank you, Paulo Coelho, for your imaginative narrative and the depth of your character development. Your ability to combine mystical themes with human experiences has been a source of inspiration for me. Your novels, particularly "The Alchemist," taught me the value of following one's dreams and listening to one's heart. Your beautiful language and philosophical insights have inspired me.

Thank you, Chimamanda Ngozi Adichie. Your fascinating storytelling and rich cultural tales have been a tremendous source of inspiration. Her work, "Half of a Yellow Sun," exemplifies how narrative can enlighten conflicting viewpoints and provide profound insights into the intricacies of our world. Adichie's real and emotionally moving novels have motivated me to approach my own work with a new understanding of the different experiences that define my life. Her dedication to capture the diverse character of the human experience has inspired me to embrace complexity in my storytelling and to truly connect with the voices and tales that enrich our world.

Thank you, Austin Kleon, for your unique viewpoint on creation and for inspiring me to share my experience with the world. Your books, including "Steal Like an Artist," have taught me that even my personal experiences and stories are worth sharing. You've taught me that creativity is more about being real than just being creative. Your guidance on accepting and expanding on one's inspirations has given me the courage to combine my own voice with the voices of people who have influenced me.

Thank you, Khalil Gibran, for your inspirational work and insightful insights into the human condition. Your poetry and intellectual writings, especially "The Prophet," have moved me deeply and broadened my awareness of life's intricacies. Your ability to impart profound insight in simple yet powerful language has affected my approach to writing, inspiring me to seek beauty and truth in every word. Your ageless teachings of love, faith, and humanity continue to connect with me and inspire my creativity.

These writers, and many more I haven't included, have influenced not just my writing but also my life with their wisdom and creativity. Their works have served as both inspiration and a reminder of literature's immense power. I am deeply thankful for their impact, which has enabled me to establish my own voice and share my tales with the world.

Finally, I want to express my heartfelt thanks, honour, and praise to the Most High God, whose limitless kindness and blessings have made everything possible. His divine providence has led and nourished me along my journey, and it is by His grace that I have arrived at this point in my life. His constant support has fulfilled my heart's desires while giving me the courage and vigour to endure. I am continuously encouraged by His presence and happy for the chance to praise and adore Him, my Lord and Saviour, Jesus Christ. Amen.

Chapter 1: A World Painted in Struggle

Within the humble walls of his room, Lesedi stood in front of a broken mirror that was hung on the wall that had been exposed to the forces of nature. He met the gaze of his own reflection, and his eyes, which were deep and introspective, echoed the soul that was within him—a spirit that desired to break free from the confines of Sebokeng, Zone 7. As he gently ran his fingers over the fabric of his paint-splattered jeans, sensory evidence of the countless hours he had spent immersed in his artistic endeavors.

As he looked out of the small window that had been weathered over time and framed his cramped room, he stared out at the bustling streets of the township that stretched out in front of him. It was a reflection of a reality that inspired him and troubled him at the same time. It was an alley of brilliant chaos and passionate struggle throughout every moment. Whether it was the continuous rhythm of its bustling marketplaces or the cacophony of voices echoed down its narrow alleyways, the township throbbed with a raw vitality that permeated into the very essence of Lesedi.

At the young age of twenty-three, he radiated a relentless passion despite the constant challenges. His creative drive was consumed with an intensity that rivaled the scorched sun above, an unyielding passion that would not be extinguished. He understood the deep significance of artistic expression, and how it can go beyond the boundaries of his surroundings and deeply resonate with people here and far beyond.

Despite the challenges he faced, he was able to see opportunities. He embraced the difficulties and challenges that surrounded him and found inspiration in their presence. Captivated by the beauty of the world, he found inspiration in every little thing around him. The worn mirror, every peeling coat of paint on the walls, and the stories etched on the faces of the people, all activated his imaginative mind. His paintings were filled with a sense of authenticity as if they were vessels for unspoken stories that longed to be told.

With strong will within his gaze, he was certain that his journey would lead him to places far beyond the limits of his hometown. Inspired by the belief that his art could go beyond limits, bridge disintegrates, and inspire change, his ambitions soared. Sebokeng was the place where he honed his craft, where he experimented with his dreams and turned them into reality. He found the fuel to take him on, to carve a road through the world with dazzling strokes of his imagination, and it was in Sebokeng's vivid chaos and hopeless fight that he located fuel to carry him forward.

And so, with a heart full of hope and a paintbrush in hand, Lesedi stepped out of his room, ready to face another day.

Sebokeng called out to him, a source of inspiration and a test, and urged him to make an everlasting impression on its fabric and to fulfill the ever-burning desire that fueled his passion.

A homogeneous array of houses lined the narrow streets, their vibrant facades stood in stark contrast to the hidden hardships and struggles within. Lesedi's upbringing had unfolded in this place—a landscape where optimism and desolation intertwined, their interplay shaped the lives of its inhabitants. In the face of overwhelming circumstances, Lesedi refused to let them limit his aspirations. He was determined to break free from the grip of poverty, never allowed his dreams to fade away.

In the tiny space he called his own, Lesedi had managed to create a peaceful haven, a place where the noise and commotion of the township seemed to disappear. Immersed in this realm of boundless creativity, his mind wandered unrestrained, liberated from the confines of the tangible world. Each little corner of the room exuded a sense of intention, carefully arranged to cater to his creative passion.

A sturdy wooden table, showing the marks of time and use, stood confidently at the heart of the room. The surface of it bore the marks of countless artistic endeavours, a testament to the love and commitment that Lesedi poured into his artistic endeavors. The table was adorned with upright brushes of varying sizes, each one ready to dance its bristles over the canvas. Colourful tubes of paint lay in a beautiful chaos, bursting with energy and creativity, each one ready to dance its bristles over the canvas. Stacks of canvases stood watch over Lesedi like patient guardians, calling for him to bring life to their blank surfaces.

In tune with his innermost being, a profound connection was established between his soul and the canvas with every stroke of his brush. As if Lesedi's own being had been transformed into rich colours and complex patterns, his spirit seemed to permeate the canvas. The unsaid thoughts, desires, and ambitions he wished to convey were given form by his brush, which he used as an emotional conduit.

It was inside the confines of this humble space that Lesedi discovered both consolation and freedom. This was the place where he was able to overcome the constraints that the harsh reality of living in Sebokeng had placed upon him. Within this realm, he found freedom from the limitations of scarcity and the weight of his circumstances. Instead, he embraced his dreams and aspirations, allowing them to come to life on the canvas before him.

Creating art within these four walls was a deeply thrilling experience for Lesedi. Time appeared to freeze as he became fully absorbed in the delicate brushstrokes and graceful patterns that slowly came together to create a captivating masterpiece. Immersed in this intimate realm, he experienced a profound sense of vitality, intertwined with the limitless potential that art encompassed.

In the solitude of his room, Lesedi discovered solace from the outside world, a solace that nourished his soul and ignited the fire within him. Here, he found solace from the suffocating clutches of lack and the unyielding challenges of the community. Like a brilliant artist, he soared above the drawbacks of his situation. In this small room, Lesedi's creativity thrived, emanating with a vibrant energy that reached exceptional heights that stretched far beyond the boundaries that confined him.

Here, the mundane became extraordinary, and thoughts, desires, and dreams soared through the brilliance of his creative expression. It was a powerful demonstration of the strength of the human spirit—to turn challenges into opportunities, limitations into freedom, and scarcity into plenty.

In the solitude of his room, Lesedi uncovered the very core of his existence. It was a place where the fire of his passion burned brightest, where his deepest desires would be given shape and form, and where he would find the most fulfillment. The modest area transformed into a sacred place, a symbol of his artistic odyssey, a reminder of the limitless possibilities that dwelled within him. Within these walls, Lesedi's artistry soared beyond the earthly realm and embraced the ethereal.

As Lesedi's brush moved gracefully across the canvas, his thoughts occasionally wandered to another constant pillar of support in his life: his mother. In his chaotic existence, her unshakable strength and gentle demeanour had always been a guiding light for him to follow. Even during times of limited resources and overwhelming challenges that could have easily dampened their aspirations, she had always been a steadfast supporter of his artistic endeavours.

She had been a supporter of his artistic endeavours since the beginning. In his mind, he recalled the numerous evenings that she devoted to sewing, with only a single bulb providing illumination. It was all in the pursuit of providing him with the necessary materials for his creations that her tired hands never wavered in their determination to do so. With each stroke of his brush, her love and unyielding determination imbued his artwork with a profound sense of meaning. Her sacrifices were intricately intertwined with each and every stroke of his brush. Lesedi found a profound source of hope and strength that permeated his work, imbuing it with an indefatigable spirit. This discovery gave Lesedi the feeling of having a muse that was inspirational.

In the midst of the difficulties and challenges that the township was experiencing, Lesedi found comfort and motivation in the steady presence of his mother, Kgalalelo. She was a powerful and resilient individual who defied the odds and refused to be broken by the difficulties they faced. She exemplified remarkable courage and fortitude. Kgalalelo put in a lot of hard work every day to provide for her family, and she did so with unyielding determination, despite the challenges that the township presented. On the other hand, her determination was not the only quality that characterised her.

The natural talent that her son possessed was something that Kgalalelo had a profound appreciation for, and she had unwavering faith in his artistic abilities. With relentless dedication, she tended to the fire of imagination that was blazing within him. She saw the fire that was burning within him. She encouraged Lesedi to enthusiastically embrace his passion for art and to pursue it with relentless dedication from the very beginning of their relationship.

When Lesedi was experiencing feelings of self-doubt, it was Kgalalelo's firm voice that reverberated deep within him, providing him with a sense of strength and certainty. It was her steadfast support that served as the impetus that propelled him forward, motivating him to triumph over his own uncertainties and constraints. In the same way that an artist is inspired by an unyielding muse, he was able to feel her unwavering faith coursing through his being, which enabled him to triumph over his uncertainties and strive for greatness.

Not only did Kgalalelo's steadfast support and unwavering faith in her son serve as a constant source of reassurance throughout his journey, but it also served as a source of fuel for his efforts to achieve his goals. In the same way that an illuminating author would, Lesedi found a source of resiliency and unshakable faith in the steadfast support of his loved one, which strengthened his resolve even in the most difficult of times. She served as a source of motivation for him, guiding him in the direction of his goals and enabling him to realize his full potential. As they made their way through the narrow streets of Sebokeng, mother and son traveled together in perfect harmony. Their connection was unshakeable, and their shared aspirations shone a light on the darkness that surrounded them. Lesedi was motivated to overcome the constraints that were placed upon him by Kgalalelo's belief, and he envisioned a future that was more than just a continuation of their humble beginnings.

Thabo, much like an experienced guide, provided Lesedi with valuable direction throughout his life. Thabo had taken on the role of a fatherly figure since their father had left many years ago. Through his profound insights and nurturing spirit, he motivated Lesedi to break free from the limitations that were imposed upon them. Thabo always told Lesedi that he could change the world through his art because he saw his boundless capabilities. The stories of artists who had triumphed over significant challenges in order to achieve success in the art world were frequently told by him. Lesedi was struck by the profound impact that Thabo's words had on him, and they motivated him to work towards his own personal development and improvement. His guidance and inspiration were truly remarkable. He was a remarkable source.

On the other hand, within the confines of their humble abode, a gloomy presence served as a constant reminder of the harsh realities that plagued the community and made their way into their lives. Jabulani, Lesedi's stepfather, battled his inner demons and found solace in the lulling fog of alcohol. His terrible inner conflicts were visible in his drunken rants and outbursts of rage, which left an indelible mark on the delicate structure of their lives. In the realm of their shared space, a feeling of fear and uncertainty permeated the walls, while the aspirations and desires of the family were intertwined with the walls.

The relationship that Lesedi had with Jabulani was a never-ending struggle against the negative influences that loomed over his goals and ambitions. Even though the destructive force of Jabulani's addiction threatened to undermine Lesedi's resilience, his relentless determination to pursue his artistic dreams remained unaffected. When Lesedi was in a state of intoxication, insensitive words were spoken with the intention of undermining his sense of self-confidence and planting the seeds of uncertainty that would later haunt him when he was in a vulnerable state.

Lesedi's memories were plagued by the lingering presence of his absent biological father, which resulted in a profound emotional void within him. Lesedi was motivated to move forward, determined to conquer the void that existed within him by pursuing remarkable accomplishments and achieving genuine success. He was inspired by the profound depths of human emotion, which inspired him to proceed. It ignited a fire within him, which fueled his determination to prove his worth not only to society but also to the elusive image of his father, who had left them.

In the face of these challenges, Lesedi discovered comfort and strength through the steadfast support of his mother, Kgalalelo. She exuded an indefatigable strength, a steadfast devotion to her son's talent. Kgalalelo's steadfast belief in Lesedi's capabilities offered a sense of stability amidst the chaos that filled their household. Just like a compassionate soul, Kgalalelo provided comfort and support to Lesedi and Thabo, protecting them from the harsh impact of Jabulani's actions. Her indefatigable love and relentless support became his guiding light, giving him the strength to persevere through the turbulent challenges they faced.

In the midst of the turmoil and the flickering shadows that filled their dwelling, Lesedi's unyielding resolve blazed with intensity. He was determined to shape his own destiny, refusing to let negativity hold him back. Inspired by the wisdom of great authors, and painters, he found strength in the face of adversity. Every painful word and destructive act caused by addiction only fueled his determination to transcend his situation and demonstrate his true worth. The challenges he faced became a powerful force that propelled him toward personal growth and inner strength.

In the face of adversity, Lesedi found solace in the close relationships he had with his mother, brother, and a handful of supportive relatives and friends who saw his true potential. Inspired by the profound faith of those around him, a ray of hope emerged amidst the prevailing scepticism, illuminating moments of uncertainty. They were his guiding lights, providing stability in the midst of chaos and fueling his belief in his own potential and the boundless opportunities that awaited him.

In the depths of his own abode, Lesedi gracefully manoeuvred through the complexities of his connections—a fragile balance between optimism and letdown, affection, and anguish. The challenges he encountered within the boundaries of his family dynamics played a significant role in shaping his journey of self-development. Every obstacle he faced, whether it was the toxic influence of Jabulani or the absence of his father, only fueled his determination, sparking an unflagging quest for success and self-discovery.

In a manner reminiscent of the journey of many renowned painters, the obstacles he encountered developed into a potent force that fueled his personal growth and inner fortitude.

Lesedi was able to find comfort in the close relationships he had with his mother, brother, and a small group of supportive relatives and friends who recognised his true potential. These relationships helped him make it through difficult times. In the midst of the prevalent scepticism, a glimmer of hope emerged, shedding light on moments of uncertainty. This was possible because he was inspired by the profound faith of those around him. They were his guiding lights, providing stability in the midst of chaos and fueling his belief in his own potential and the limitless opportunities that awaited him. They were his guiding lights.

Lesedi was able to deftly navigate the complexities of his connections while concealed within the confines of his own home. He maintained a delicate equilibrium between optimism and letdown, affection and anguish while doing so. The difficulties that he encountered within the confines of his family dynamics played a significant role in shaping his journey of self-development. Every challenge he encountered, whether it was the poisonous influence of Jabulani or the absence of his father, served only to strengthen his resolve and ignite an unyielding pursuit of success and self-discovery.

It seemed apparent to Lesedi that the path leading to the realization of his goals would not be an easy one.

There was a wide range of thoughts and opinions that were present among Lesedi's friends and family who were a part of his social circle. Many believed in his creative ability and stood by him as staunch followers, admiring his evident genius. Inspired by the constant support of others, he was set on beating the chances that were against him.

On the other hand, several individuals did not have the same degree of faith in Lesedi's capabilities. A number of individuals had a difficult time accepting the notion that a young black man from the township of Sebokeng could achieve such a prominent position in the world of art. Because of their limited worldviews and the impact of society, they were unable to see Lesedi overcoming the difficult conditions that were present in their environment. His objectives were thrown in a shadow of uncertainty as a result of their own, which were affected by their own cultural and social perceptions.

Lesedi's ears were filled with the echoes of doubt, which were weighed down by the weight of centuries of inequity and restrictions that were imposed by the system. His statements struck a chord deep within him, calling into question the tenacity of his determination and causing him to question the shaky foundations of his goals and ambitions. Those ideas reverber-ated throughout him, planting seeds of uncertainty that were designed to damage his sense of self-assurance.

Despite the doubts of others, Lesedi continued to be resolute in his ambition to forge his own path, despite the fact that others were skeptical. He came to the realisation that their uncertainty was not a result of his personal talents or potential, but rather of the limitations that society had set on their collective imagi-nation. Having a perspective that was impacted by a society that had not yet completely appreciated his creative genius, he knew that their doubt was the source of their uncertainty.

Lesedi's willpower got greater as a result of their uncertainty because of their doubts. Their doubt was absorbed by him, and he used it as a source of energy to fuel his desire. He turned his uncertainties into stepping stones, which served as a tool to demonstrate that they were incorrect. He had a great capacity to transcend the limitations of ordinary imagination and produce works that left observers in wonder. This skill gave him a significant advantage in the area of artistic craftsmanship.

The great self-confidence that Lesedi had shined brilliantly, shielding him from the uncertainties that had the potential to make his dreams not come true. He had the understanding that in order to achieve success, it was necessary to confront obstacles and problems head-on. With an unyielding determination to break through the limitations that had been holding him back and leave an indelible mark on the world of art, he was motivated by the greats who had come before him and inspired by their achievements.

Lesedi's mission was crystal clear—he had an insatiable desire to become a successful artist, determined to silence all those who had ever doubted him. He desired to build a magnificent home for his mother, a haven shielded from the harshness of the township. He wanted to break free from the oppressive hold of poverty, to paint his future with colorful strokes of prosperity and financial comfort. Inspired by the wisdom of great creators, Lesedi stood at the threshold of a world yet to be painted, ready to embrace the unknown with a heart brimming with hope and an indefatigable spirit.

Stepping out into the energetic streets of Sebokeng, Lesedi was surrounded by a symphony of sounds. The joyful laughter of children filled the air as they played in the dirt, while the rhythmic beats of drums resonated from the nearby community centre. The vibrant conversations of market vendors bargaining over their goods added to the lively atmosphere. It was a world filled with vibrant existence, yet burdened by the hardships of poverty and adversity. The exterior surfaces of the shack houses were adorned with a vibrant array of colours, reflecting a spirit of fortitude that contrasted sharply with the harshness of their surroundings.

Lesedi has always been captivated by the enchanting world of colors—their mesmerising dance, harmonious blending, and their ability to express emotions into tangible forms. He saw potential in every colour, as if each one held a hidden tale. Immersed in a world of inspiration, the sights, sounds, and stories beckoned to him, yearning to be captured and brought to life through his art. He understood that hidden within the challenges and difficulties, there was a profound beauty yearning to be discovered—a beauty that only he possessed the power to awaken.

Every day, Lesedi was drawn to the heart of the township, his trusty sketchbook held tightly in his hands—a constant companion on his artistic adventures. Like a masterful observer, he embarked on a journey, navigating the intricate pathways of the town while fully attuned to the vibrant tapestry of life that unfolded before him.

Immersed in the very nature of Sebokeng's existence, Lesedi became an empathetic witness, deciphering the vibrant rhythm of its pulsating life. In the midst of the packed trade markets, he would always manage to find a quiet corner. Whether it was a weathered wooden stool or the weathered wall of a vendor's stall, he would find his spot. There, with his reliable pencil in hand, he would skillfully capture the true spirit of Sebokeng and its inhabitants.

His sketchbook shaped into windows into the lives of his neighbors—the aged faces marked by the passage of time, their features carved with tales of strength and endurance. Lesedi's pencil skillfully glided across the paper, skillfully capturing the lines and shadows that brought their features to life. Every stroke intended to encapsulate their unique essence, to preserve the emotions that danced in their gaze and the wisdom engraved on their faces.

Through his art, Lesedi breathed life into Sebokeng's vibrancy. He captured the vibrant energy of the bustling market, transforming it into a masterpiece of art. His sketches turned into a beautiful visual story, delicately bringing together broken pieces of optimism discovered often hidden within the persistent battle of struggle.

Inspired by the spirit of life, Lesedi breathed vitality into his sketches, capturing the essence of joy and strength that echoed through the winding streets. In his quest, he aimed to uncover the hidden beauty, the intricate dance between power and fragility that resided in every nook and cranny of the township. Every sketch captured the relentless resilience of its people, a tribute to their capacity to discover happiness in the face of hardship.

Lesedi's sketches possess a profound ability to not only depict the physical appearance of his subjects, but also to convey the rich narratives that lie within—their victories, their sorrows, their aspirations, and the serene instances of relentless determination. With his art, he sought to strengthen their voices, visually represent their stories, and connect them with the rest of the world.

As he explored further into the township, his sketchbook became a vibrant collection of faces, market scenes, and snapshots of daily existence. Every sketch was a stroke on the grand canvas of his artistic voyage—a testament to the profound impact of keen observation, deep empathy, and the boundless capacity of art to surpass limitations.

Lesedi persisted in his artistic pursuit, skillfully immortalising the essence of the township on the pages of his sketchbook. He used his art to champion the cause of those who are often overlooked, silenced, and yet, remarkably strong. In his sketches, he aimed to awaken empathy and encourage others to recognise the hidden beauty and resilience within every community.

Flipping through the pages of his sketchbook, he felt a sense of accomplishment, knowing that he had fulfilled his mission for the day. The township's beauty, as depicted in his sketches, emanated with a serene strength—a gentle reminder that hope, even amidst adversity, could be discovered in the most surprising corners.

And as Lesedi's talent blossomed, his dreams extended far beyond the boundaries of the township. He longed for his work to be recognised on a larger scale, and to have the opportunity to showcase it in prestigious venues where art was truly valued and celebrated. He imagined his works gracing the walls of esteemed galleries, stirring emotions, and igniting discussions that transcended the boundaries of the local community. He longed to surpass the limitations of his modest origins and leave a lasting impression in the expansive realm of art.

Deeply immersed in their work, Lesedi passionately expressed his innermost self through each brushstroke and every burst of colour on the canvas. His artistic expression went beyond capturing images; it transformed into a deep reflection of his own journey. With a touch of artistry, it captured the essence of his life's journey, the dreams he pursued, and the challenges he faced head-on.

In spite of the fact that Lesedi seemed to be extremely motivated, subtle self-doubt was eating away at the very core of his being. Every moment of the day, he was constantly reminded of the voices of those who did not believe he was capable of handling the current circumstances. One could feel the weight of their uncertainty hanging in the air, ready to chip away at his sense of self-assurance. Lesedi was conscious of the need to overcome these doubts, soar above the paralyzing uncertainty, and prove to himself and the rest of the world that his path was one that was meant to end in amazing success. Despite this, Lesedi was aware of the need to overcome these uncertainties.

Unexpected happenings were about to unfold as Lesedi set off to face these obstacles on his path to creative development and self-discovery.

He had an acute awareness of the uncertainty that surrounded him, the whispers that mocked him and said things like, "You'll never succeed." Yet, these doubts only served to ignite his passion, propelling him to challenge the limitations set by both society and his environment. His determination to prove his value deepened as time went on. He saw the world as an infinite wellspring of ideas, a place where his fantasies and the world around him brought together to create a colorful tapestry of works.

His painting studio was a hallowed space where he could reshape his surroundings, where each brushstroke represented victory over adversity and sorrow. He sought peace in his art studio. In every single picture, he built a narrative that portrayed the power of perseverance, hope, and the extraordinary potential of desires. While Lesedi was in the thick of the difficulties that the township was experiencing, he came into a source of tremendous inspiration. As a result of being influenced by the environment around him, he discovered beauty in the most unexpected places. Through his creations, he captured the indomitable spirit and untiring strength of his community. His intention was to challenge preconceived notions and bring to light the storylines that are often ignored and that are found on the periphery.

Lesedi stood at the precipice of a vast canvas, ready to bring his artistic vision to life. The voyage that lay ahead of him would test his dedication, push the boundaries of his creative potential, and need a firm confidence in his artistic vision.

Inspired by the spirit of adventure and propelled by his unrelenting enthusiasm, Lesedi was ready to go on a journey that would test his creativity, stretch his limitations, and redefine his creative vision. All of these things would be accomplished by means of the journey. Lesedi's brush would turn into a powerful weapon, much like the brush of a great artist, and his artwork would serve as a forceful witness to the determined spirit that was inside him.

In the comforting embrace of the sun's rays, Lesedi breathed in the heady air of hope and opportunity. He let it fill his lungs. His footsteps reverberated through the bustling streets, leading him in the direction of a future that was more challenging than the ones he had previously encountered. In an effort to produce a story that was captivating, he embarked on an adventure. The narrative came to life with each stroke of his pencil, presenting a universe that didn't conform to any one image.

A little black child had the opportunity to start on a fantastic voyage in the township of Sebokeng. Through the course of this voyage, he would encounter art, self-discovery, the tenacity of the human spirit, and the enchanted power of brushstrokes, all of which would finally determine his fate. And so it came to be that Lesedi set off on an adventure into the unknown streets, fully prepared to challenge the rules of the universe, turn adversity into inspiration, and create an indelible imprint on the very fabric of his daily existence.

Chapter 2: The Palette of Dreams

In the worn-out confines of their humble dwelling, the atmosphere was burdened by the weight of a shattered life. Lesedi's family found themselves entangled in the complex structure of their own struggles, bravely dealing with the unpredictable landscape of their fracturing existence. In the dimly lit living room, Lesedi sat at the worn wooden table, his sketchbook open before him. The mellow illumination of a single bulb threw lengthy shadows around the room, showing the peeling paint on the walls and the age-worn fabric of the vintage couch.

Lesedi's mother stood by the doorway, observing her youngest son with a blend of pride and worry. Her face, inscribed with the hardships of their everyday existence, grew gentle whenever she gazed upon Lesedi. She was the rock of the family, her strength and untiring love keeping them united during the most challenging moments.

Kgalalelo's day had been exhausting and demanding. She began her mornings before sunrise, preparing her small stall in the marketplace. Like a skilled merchant, she effortlessly traded fruits and vegetables, her hands always in motion, exchanging goods and currency. The market was bustling and lively, yet Kgalalelo effortlessly manoeuvred through it, her confident voice rising above the commotion as she reached out to potential customers. Her dedication extended beyond her regular work. After her day job, she would come home and draw on her sewing skills to take on mending projects for her neighbors, earning a bit of extra cash.

Tonight, she had just arrived home, feeling drained yet fierce in her commitment to support her loved ones. Her body was tired and sore from the long hours spent standing and hunched. Her fingers were numb from the cold and the rough materials she handled. However, even though she was tired, a gentle smile appeared on her face when she noticed Lesedi fully immersed in his creative work. She found solace in witnessing the moments of peace and creativity her children discovered, despite the challenges they faced.

Thabo, Lesedi's older brother, displayed an undeniable presence, even when he wasn't physically present in the adjoining room. Thabo was Lesedi's greatest supporter, constantly encouraging him to follow his artistic passion. Thabo temporarily set aside his own dreams of pursuing a career in music. Instead, he selflessly dedicated himself to supporting his brother, Lesedi, and their mother by taking on various odd jobs to ensure their financial stability.

The sound of his stepfather's unsteady footsteps rippled through the house, as he approached the room, each one a painful reminder of the brokenness that plagued their existence. He was a ghostly presence that cast a terrible shadow over their previously bright home because he had been trapped by alcohol, which completely changed him. In the room, his mother moved with a sense of weariness mixed with determination, her eyes revealing the heaviness of their collective struggle.

As Lesedi looked up from his drawings, the aroma of alcohol wafted across the room as his stepfather staggered in. The existence of his presence was like a gloomy cloud, and it flung a shadow over their very loving home.

"Another night gone to waste," his stepfather slurred, his voice dripping with bitterness. "Do you truly believe that your drawings will save you, boy?"

His stepfather dismissed the idea, his voice filled with doubt and cynicism.

The power of his words pierced the atmosphere, resonating in the small, dimly illuminated space. His gaze, weathered by a lifetime of failures and hardships, pierced through Lesedi's, as if attempting to extinguish the flame of optimism that flickered within him.

The old man stepped nearer, his breath heavy with the scent of cheap booze, a stark reminder of the weight that burdened them all. "Do you really believe that those pointless pictures, whatever meaningless thing you call them, put food on the table or keep a roof over our heads? Look at you, wasting time on those useless scribbles while the rest of us struggle to survive. Your so-called talent is nothing but a fantasy. Do you think anyone cares about your drawings? You're living in a dream world, Lesedi. Grow up and face reality!"

He pointed forcefully at the sketches scattered across the table, each one showcasing Lesedi's immense talent and aspirations.

"You must face the truth, boy. Art has zero power to make any significant impact on this world. It's about time you matured and started doing something meaningful with a worthless life."

He clutched his sketchbook tightly, its pages full of vivid visualizations and aspirations that appeared to lose their brilliance under the intense scrutiny of his stepfather's stare. The boy's heart raced in his chest, torn between a sense of rebellion and uncertainty.

He had heard these words countless times, each instance slowly wearing down his confidence, much like the constant erosion of a once-mighty cliff by relentless waves.

"Do you really believe that your drawings can save you?" The question echoed in his thoughts, a melancholic refrain that risked overshadowing the optimism and fervor that propelled his every action.

However, despite the mocking laughter from his stepfather, Lesedi felt a flicker of resolve ignite inside him. He understood that his work was more than a hobby; it was a means of survival, a means to make sense of the mayhem and find some calm in the storm.

He looked down at the unfinished sketch in his lap, freezing at the image of his mother with her gentle gaze and a beautiful smile. He saw in her a remarkable strength and resilience that had guided them through countless challenges. Her steadfast encouragement was a powerful example of the strength of faith, a gentle push to persist despite challenges and find a path ahead.

With a calm and determined voice, Lesedi looked up at his stepfather, ready to speak.

"No, my drawings won't save us," he said, his gaze resolute.

"But they inspire a sense of hope within me. They serve as a reminder that life encompasses more than just this ongoing battle. Perhaps, there is a possibility that they can assist us in perceiving the beauty that exists within our suffering."

Lesedi's fixed gaze reflected his unbreakable spirit.

He had become familiar with these verbal attacks, yet they still managed to hurt him on a deeper level.

"Art is my haven, a source of comfort despite the struggle," he replied gently, his words tinged with a touch of rebellion. "It may not provide solutions to our hardships, but it fills me with a sense hope, that one day all is going to be well. It serves as a reminder that even in the midst of darkness, beauty can still find a way to exist."

"Hope!" His stepfather sneered, his mocking laughter echoing through the room.

"Hope alone won't provide food or pay the bills, boy. Dreams will never satisfy your hunger."

Lesedi refused to let the weight of his stepfather's words dampen his relentless determination. "I know, but art holds a deeper importance," he said, his voice filled with a restrained passion. "It's my unique voice, my way of expressing myself, and I refuse to compromise on that."

The expression on his stepfather's face contorted into a sneer, his eyes filled with fury.

"What a whiny brat you are! After all, I've done for you, this is how you show your gratitude? You are nothing without me!" He advanced with an intimidating stride, his voice growing louder with every word.

The tiny room appeared to contract, the walls pressing closer as Lesedi remained motionless, his heart thumping in his chest.

"Do you really believe your drawings are something extraordinary?" His stepfather spat, his words dripping with malice. "Whose money do you use to buy those paints and materials, huh? You think it's you who pays for them, or you think it's your mother, huh? Let me tell you if you don't know, IT'S MY MONEY!"

Before Lesedi could react, his stepfather swiftly snatched the sketchpad from his hands.

"Look at this garbage!" he exclaimed, raising the drawings in the air. "Is this how you choose to spend your time? Is this what you believe will be your salvation?"

In a cruel manner, he started to rip the pages apart, the noise of the paper being torn echoing throughout the room.

Lesedi witnessed his efforts and aspirations crumble before him, leaving him in a state of utter dismay.

"No! Please, don't!" Lesedi exclaimed, desperately reaching out.

Unfortunately, his stepfather showed no mercy, ruthlessly destroying and crumpling the drawings, letting the fragments fall to the ground like lifeless foliage. The vibrant pieces lay scattered at their feet, an unexpected dichotomy to the somberness of the occasion.

Lesedi fought back the tears that attempted to pour out of his eyes, determined not to show any weakness in front of his stepfather. He felt more defiant because of his mother's love and support and because he remembered how much his brother had helped him. He refused to let his dreams be shattered.

"I'll show to you one day," Lesedi whispered, his voice filled with a mix of fear and determination. "I'll prove that I am greater than you think of me."

Just then, Kgalalelo screamed, "Stop it, Jabulani! Leave him alone!" she exclaimed, attempting to pull the last few pages from Jabulani's grasp. Even so, Kgalalelo proved to be no match for the older man's overwhelming brute force, effortlessly shoving her aside.

"Stay out of this, Kgalalelo," their stepfather growled. "This is none of your business."

"It is my business! Lesedi is my son!" Kgalalelo shouted, her voice filled with intense emotion. She made another desperate attempt, only to be met with the same outcome.

Pushed back and rendered helpless, she could only watch as the last of Lesedi's drawings were torn apart.

Lesedi found the strength to assist his mother in his time of need. "Don't ever touch her like that!" Lesedi raised his voice, firmly gripping his stepfather's arm. However, the man's immense power proved to be too much for Lesedi, who was effortlessly brushed aside and sent crashing to the floor alongside Kgalalelo.

"Both of you, stay down!" their stepfather shouted, towering above them, his chest heaving with rage.

The words overwhelmed Lesedi, engulfing him in a sea of uncertainty. Even though his determination wavered for a brief period of time, he forced himself to maintain a steady voice. "You may support my basic needs, but that doesn't mean I am worthless or give you the right to devalue my art," he expressed, his voice filled with a sense of rebellion. "I have dreams beyond mere existence, and I refuse to let you put me down."

In a fit of rage and under the influence of alcohol, his stepfather aggressively moved closer, his words dripping with malice. "Do you think you're better than me? An artist with no talent like you will never achieve success. No matter how much you practice, your efforts will never be sufficient. No matter how much you believe in yourself, you will still be worthless in my eyes. That's the reason your father left you. He recognised the same insignificance in you that I am right now witnessing.

You're simply an unnecessary burden, imagining a life that will never come to reality. Your feeble attempts at art will have no effect whatsoever. Do you really believe that your drawings have the potential to make a meaningful the effect on society? You're fooling yourself, boy. Your future seems to lack the brightness and purpose you find in those meaningless pieces of paper you hold dear."

His eyes welling with tears, struggled to find the strength to reply. "Art is the one thing that truly gives me life. It's the one thing that fills me with joy and gives me a deep sense of purpose. Just as you do when you indulge in your kind of beverage. I seek peace in my art while you seek escape in the bottle, finding a way to get away and numb the pain. Drawing is my way of coping, similar to how everyone has their own ways, I have mine."

Jabulani's expression turned stormy with frustration. "You must never think about comparing my drinking behaviors to your meaningless drawings, young man. I face reality directly. You simply just hide behind your art, believing they have the power to bring about change."

"It gives a much-needed escape from all this... this over-whelming hopelessness. It's a way to break free from all of this."

Jabulani's expression grew even more disdainful.

"Escape?" his voice laced with biting irony. "Do you really believe that those ridiculous images will take you away from reality? Life doesn't operate in such a manner, my boy. While some of you are focused on pursuing dreams, it's important to remember that the rest of us are working hard to survive. You're living in a dream world, and it's about time you faced reality."

Kgalalelo, feeling compelled to speak up, positioned herself between Jabulani and Lesedi. "Just let him be, Jabulani! Lesedi's art has a purpose. It's a deep-seated passion, a source of joy. You can't simply dismiss that out of bitterness and anger."

Jabulani's expression contorted with anger as he faced Kgalalelo. "How dare you challenge me! You are just as delusional as he is. Both of you have failed, and are failures. Do you believe the world truly values your dreams and passions? The world can be a tough, unfair, and ruthless place. Dreams alone will not give sustenance."

Her face reflecting a blend of weariness and stubborn determination. "That's it, no more! You've expressed your thoughts enough. These boys are giving it their all. Lesedi's art holds immense significance, on par with any other endeavor. We should offer our support to them, rather than shattering their hopes and dreams."

She turns to gaze at Lesedi and says, "They must do better than us, live a more fulfilling life than we did, and build a more opulent home than the one we currently inhabit."

Jabulani shot a fierce look at Kgalalelo, his hands tightly balled into fists. "Support? Support! Is this what you think support is? Allowing him to squander his time on trivial matters while we endure hardships? You're just as oblivious as they are. This family could benefit from an understanding of reality, rather than indulging in empty dreams."

Kgalalelo, filled with determination, confronted Jabulani. "We may face challenges, but we will never give up on our dreams. Lesedi's art shines brightly amidst the darkness of this world. And we will fiercely defend the flame of hope, regardless of what you say."

Jabulani, filled with anger, surveyed the staunch expressions on the faces of his family. "You're all foolish," he exclaimed.

Lesedi's heart pounded with a surge of fear, yet he remained steadfast and firm. Even though he had been subjected to years of emotional torture, he managed to keep a spark of hope alive deep inside his essence until the very end. It was the relentless belief in his dreams that propelled him to desire to overcome his challenging situation.

He locked eyes with his stepfather, displaying a resolute and committed demeanor. "You may test my endurance in an attempt to dampen my enthusiasm, but I refuse to let it happen. I will persist in my creative endeavors, using my art as a means of self-expression, regardless of any obstacles that may arise."

Lesedi's mother stepped forward, her voice filled with a blend of exhaustion and resolve. "And dreams have the power to awaken the fire inside, granting us the strength to persevere," she expressed, her gaze fixed on her son's. "Lesedi's art is his true passion, a remarkable talent that sets him apart. It's what drives him forward, even when faced with challenges."

His stepfather's eyes gleamed with fury as he wavered uncertainly. "Passion won't provide sustenance either," he said with disdain, his speech slurred. "You're raising him to be a dreamer, a fool."

Lesedi's older brother, Thabo, appeared from the darkness, exuding an aura of authority and tranquility. "There's more to life than just surviving," he declared with conviction, his voice offering solace amidst the gathering tempest. "Lesedi's art shines brightly, serving as a constant reminder of the beauty that exists in this world and the importance of fighting for it."

His words lingered in the atmosphere, delicately balancing between optimism and desolation. Lesedi's pencil hovered above the sketchbook, his fingers eager to bring his inner emotions to life through his art.

"I will continue to dream, regardless of the world's discouragement," Lesedi declared, his voice fixed and determined. "Through my art, I shall be able to overcome the limitations of this broken life. I will create a brighter tomorrow for everyone in this place."

His stepfather scoffed once more, his voice filled with resentment, he spat, before storming out of the room. "You're all foolish," he whispered, forcefully closing the door and vanishing into the darkness.

In the heavy silence that followed, Kgalalelo turned to Lesedi, placing a reassuring hand on his shoulder. "Don't listen to him, Lesedi. Your art matters. It matters to me, to your brother, and most importantly, it matters to you."

Lesedi's mother enveloped her son in a warm embrace, her touch radiating a love that transcended language. "Keep dreaming, my son," she whispered, her voice exuding a serene determination. "May your art serve as a testament to our indefatigable strength, to the radiance that persists even amidst adversity."

Inspired by the words of his mother, Lesedi immersed himself in his sketches, his pencil effortlessly flowing across the paper. In the depths of their humble abode, he discovered comfort in his artistic pursuits, a haven where imagination could soar and where pain could be transmuted into something exquisite.

* * *

As the golden rays of the evening light began to set in, giving a warm and compassionate glow to the world outside, Lesedi situated himself in a peaceful corner of the family room. His sketchbook rested gently on his lap, ready to be animated by the touch of his pencil, infusing its empty pages with vibrant life. Like an observer in the shadows, his mother, tired yet unyielding, observed him with eyes that contained a blend of sadness and optimism. In the depths of her being, she bore the weight of their shattered household, sensing the heaviness of her spouse's hardships weighing on her spirit. However, she also witnessed the glowing flame of imaginative thinking that blazed inside her son, a glimmer that had the potential to rise above their difficult situation.

"Lesedi," she whispered gently, her voice tinged with weariness yet filled with resolute determination,

"I understand the scope of the difficulties that lie before us. We are all haunted by the demons that plague your stepfather. However, my beloved child, you have been blessed with a special talent. Your art is a ticket, a sanctuary where your spirit can reach beyond the chaos that surrounds us, and will take us with you, into a better future, I trust you, my boy."

Lesedi raised his eyes from the sketchbook and made eye contact with his mother. Witnessing a deep love in her aged face, marked by sacrifice and perseverance, left a lasting impression on him. He understood the profound extent of her trust in his talents, the unshakeable confidence she had in his power to create their future together.

"Mama," he whispered, his voice filled with a yearning, "I am determined to shape my own reality. In my artistic endeavors, I really desire to create a future filled with hope and bravery, not just for me, but for our entire family."

His mother's eyes glistened with unspoken sadness as she nodded, her voice vibrating with deep emotions. "My dear son, I have faith in you. You possess a brilliance that shines brightly amidst the chaos of life. It's a powerful reminder that even in the darkest moments, beauty can still find its way to the surface."

There was an unspoken connection formed in that fleeting instant, connecting their hearts through common understanding. Lesedi's stepfather loomed in the background, a haunting reminder of their hardships. Despite everything that had happened to them, they found comfort in the bonds of family and the life-altering potential of creative expression.

As Lesedi's pencil gracefully moved across the sketchbook's canvas, he poured his heart and soul onto the pages, capturing the delicate balance between sorrow and joy that resided within their home. Every brushstroke became a testament to their unshakeable strength, a powerful declaration that their indomitable spirits would never be silenced.

Approaching him with a gentle grace, his mother's voice became a soft murmur of encouragement. "Lesedi, my son, your art has the power to bring healing to our broken home and touch the hearts of those who experience its essence. You have the power to awaken a spark in others, motivating them to rise above their challenges."

In a manner reminiscent of great artists before him, Lesedi wholeheartedly embraced the burden of their shattered existence, using it as inspiration to fuel his creative passion. Inspired by the profound love of his mother and influenced by the complex presence of his stepfather, he set out on a quest to create a story that would deeply touch the souls of countless individuals.

In the cozy sanctuary of Lesedi's bedroom, the moonlight cast a soft light into Lesedi's bedroom, which was already filled with the artifacts of his youth as well as the burden of his unspoken sorrows. Taking a seat at his desk, sat with his sketchbook open in front of him. The pages of the sketchbook offered an oasis for his ideas and dreams. The atmosphere reeked of an unpleasant conversation that had taken place earlier on, an exchange marked by emotional abuse and harsh language that kept on echoing uncomfortably.

Thabo, the wise older brother, stood casually in the doorway, offering solace to Lesedi's bruised soul. They had a deep connection, a bond that went beyond words, built on their shared experiences and mutual commitment to each other's well-being. Thabo's intense gaze met Lesedi's, reflecting a potent mix of concern and determination. Lesedi, momentarily distracted from his sketches, displayed uncertainty in his eyes.

"What burdens your soul, my dearest brother?" Thabo's voice, gentle yet authoritative, pierced the stillness, resonating within the depths of Lesedi's being.

Lesedi, with a firm hold on the pencil, paused briefly, reflecting on the significance of his desires and the emotional wounds inflicted by their stepfather's cruelty. His voice quivered with a sensitive blend of openness and resistance as he bared his soul.

"The challenges we encounter, the anguish that lingers within our home...It's very heavy on my soul, but I am compelled by an immense desire to express it all, to creatively express the narratives hidden within every aspect of our being, I want to comfort those who have endured in silence, ensuring that their stories are never forgotten, and that they not alone."

Thabo, with a deep sense of pride and wisdom, drew nearer to Lesedi, offering a reassuring presence that provided solace in the face of encroaching shadows. "Your sketches have an unparalleled strength and beauty, dear brother,"

Thabo whispered, his voice filled with unyielding belief. "With every stroke, there is a profound power to reach the depths of souls, awakening long-forgotten emotions. It is important to keep in mind that the responsibilities of the world cannot be placed solely on your shoulders."

Lesedi's eyes were ablaze with a newly discovered sense of purpose, and he reached for the pencil with a renewed sense of determination. His voice was filled with conviction.

"I want to have an impact that is significant, Thabo. Just like renowned artists and great people before, I aspire to create something extraordinary with my art, to bring light to the darkness that surrounds us in our broken home and the community we live in.

Thabo's eyes softened, a sense of quiet admiration emanating from his every word, as if he, too, recognised the spark of brilliance within his younger brother.

"You have an incredible future ahead of you, Lesedi," Thabo assured, his voice filled with a calm yet compelling strength. "It is important to continue to keep in mind that true greatness is not solely measured by the accomplishment of one's own desires, but also by the ability to inspire and support others on their own journeys. Embrace the power of your art to inspire hope and ignite transformation."

As Lesedi's eyes gleamed with a newfound sense of determination, Thabo, always there as a reliable source of support, gently placed a hand on his brother's shoulder, a silent expression of deep affection and steadfast dedication.

"Rest assured, Lesedi, we are here by your side," Thabo comforted, his voice filled with gentle support. "Your art has the power to change lives, starting with our own." Lesedi nodded, a determined smile appearing on his lips as if the gravity of the conversation had dissipated, leaving behind a glimmer of resolve.

"I won't allow our challenges to shape who we are," Lesedi

declared, his voice filled with determination. "Together, we will rise above them, and someday, our dreams will become bound together with the very essence of life."

As the soft moonlight fills the room with its gentle radiance, Lesedi redirects his attention to the sketchbook, ready to capture the essence of their conversation with his poised pencil. In the quietude that fills the space, a sense of optimism and determination merge, creating a glimpse of a forthcoming altered by their steadfast faith.

With his artistic talents and the unyielding support of his loved ones, he fearlessly awaits to face the obstacles that await him. The beginning of Lesedi's artistic journey can be traced back to the walls of their humble home, and the echoes of their brokenness. The movement of his pencil across the pages was like a dance, transforming the darkness into light and the pain into beauty. Like a masterful storyteller, art reshaped into a powerful catalyst, uniting their fragmented existence with the boundless realm of endless potential. Lesedi and his family clung to their hope, firmly convinced that even in the bleakest moments, the magic of art and the power of their love could guide them toward a brighter future.

***

The next day began with a vivid array of potential. Lesedi woke up early, his mind filled with the conversations that had taken place the night before. He felt a complex blend of emotions, a tapestry of inspiration woven from sadness and hope. Carrying his sketchbook, he ventured to the front yard and prepared his easel, feeling a profound connection to the world outside their troubled abode.

As Lesedi perched on a weathered wooden stool, his pencil poised above the empty canvas, he aimed to capture the profound connection of their heartfelt conversation. As he started to carve fine lines, bringing physical form to the thoughts and feelings that had lingered in his spirit, his hands quivered with excitement. Each stroke carried the weight of their collective struggles, but it also carried the glimmer of fortitude that resisted being snuffed by everything that happened.

Immersed in his creation, Lesedi was captivated by the cascading morning sunlight. Immersed in his art, the world around him faded away, his pencil moving with a delicate balance of skill and emotion. As the picture took shape, it became a moving representation of the journey that their family had taken; it was a mosaic of brokenness and healing, hopelessness and joy.

As the day went on, Lesedi's art captivated the attention of those around him, attracting neighbors and passersby who were eager to witness the creation of his masterpiece. Every interaction carried a profound significance, a bond intricately intertwined within the intricate work of his artistry. In the quiet of the evening, the elderly widow from next door greeted Lesedi with a gentle smile and kind words. Her eyes held a wealth of knowledge, as she whispered words of encouragement in a voice that exuded warmth.

Looking up from his painting, the artist glanced around and smiled warmly. "Good evening, Gogo Mkhize. How are you feeling today?"

Seated on a nearby bench, her movements are unhurried, just elegant. "I'm doing fine, my dear. Your painting caught my attention. It is truly impressive. You possess a remarkable talent,

Lesedi."

With a hint of a blush, he glanced at his work and said, "Thank you, Gogo Mkhize. I'm simply attempting to convey my observations and emotions."

Bending in more closely, her wise eyes sparkled with knowledge, "I've seen a great deal over my life, both good and bad. Your art... it reflects all, and resonates with all people. It evokes a sense of the profound beauty and strength that dwells within our local area, within our fellow human race."

His eyes widened as he felt the impact of what she said, "Do you truly believe that, Gogo? There are moments when I have the impression that they are little more than meaningless scribbles."

"Oh, Lesedi, every brushstroke you create is filled with a part of your soul. Your art has the power to allow people to see the world through your unique perspective. Never underestimate the strength of your voice."

With a nod of affirmation, feeling a surge of motivation, "I will, Gogo Mkhize. Thanks a lot. I deeply appreciate the profoundness of your encouraging words."

With a warm smile, "I have experienced numerous years and witnessed a multitude of things, my dear. Have faith in your talent and keep spreading it to the world. You never know whose life you might deeply impact."

With a smile, "I will, Gogo Mkhize. I give you my word."

As, Gogo Mkhize, gently stood up, she commented, "Good. Now, continue to create, my brilliant boy. The way you see things is a gift that the world deserves to take joy in experiencing."

As he watched her gracefully retreat into her home, a surge of determination washed over him. Under his breath, he murmured, "I will, Gogo. I will."

A group of kids, their laughter filling the air with joy, gathered around him, their eyes filled with awe. Inspired by the works of Lesedi's artwork that captivated a mind and stimulated their own desires in the world of art. They bombarded him with questions, their vibrant energy igniting his own fervor. At that very moment, he had a profound realisation of the deep impact that his art could have on the lives of others, particularly those who had lost all hope.

Thandi, leaning in to examine the painting, asked Lesedi about his technique for achieving such lifelike colors, "It's as if the people are about to come alive from the canvas!"

Lesedi, with a smile on his face, delicately dips his brush into a palette of vibrant paint, "Seeing the world in your own special way is what truly matters, Thandi. Colours are more than just what you see. They also affect how you feel. There is a story behind every stroke."

Neo exclaimed with excitement, "I also want to paint! And tell my stories with color, and make a beautiful story. Can you show us how to do it?"

Lesedi laughed, "Sure thing, Neo. Art has the power to touch the hearts of all people. You only need a little thought and a lot of love."

Lebo's eyes are filled with a sense of awe and curiosity, "Can I bring my dreams to life through art? My mind is filled with countless!"

Lesedi nodded, offering his encouragement. "Yes, Lebo. Draw your hopes, fears, and happiness. Making art is a great way to express yourself."

Anelisa, with a pensive look on her face, asked "Lesedi, What inspires you to paint? What do you want to show them?"

Lesedi pauses, gazing at the children with a serious yet gentle expression. "I paint because it's my way of expressing myself," he said. "At times, mere words fall short in capturing the depths of our emotions. Our lives, our struggles, and our joys are what I wish to show. My desire is to encourage people to find value in sharing their own personal narratives, especially, telling African stories."

Thandi exclaims, "I would love to experience that as well! I want to share my innermost thoughts and emotions through creating art, sharing with others the unique world that resides within me."

Lesedi's smile radiates warmth, "Then begin today, you are still young, Thandi. Begin by observing your surroundings and connecting with your inner emotions. Every aspiring artist begins their journey with a sparkle of curiosity and a dream."

Taking out a stick and acting like a painter, Sam replied, "Let's paint the world, Lesedi!"

Lesedi, filled with laughter, is brimming with hope and inspiration. "Yes, Sam. Together, we can paint the world."

* * *

As the sun started to set, casting elongated shadows across the garden, Lesedi's heart filled with a mix of contentment and longing. He had dedicated his heart and soul to the artwork, yet it remained unfinished, mirroring the ongoing journey they all embarked upon. His gaze swept across the people surrounding him, taking in the deep insight and strength reflected in their faces.

In the dimming glow, an older gentleman, with a leisurely pace yet a vibrant soul, approached Lesedi. His face showed the signs of a long journey, his eyes reflecting the depth of experience. "Young man," he said with a wise smile, "sometimes the true beauty lies in the brushstrokes that are left unfinished. Your work beautifully captures the essence of the human experience. Embrace the flaws, as they reflect the intricacies of existence."

Lesedi nodded, deeply moved by the wisdom of the elderly man. He had experienced a multitude of encounters throughout the day, which had left him feeling enriched with inspiration and wisdom. In the depths of nightfall, he hesitantly put aside his incomplete work of art, aware that it would forever symbolize their unending voyage.

Channeling the spirits of great artists before him, Lesedi gently shut his sketchbook, preserving the rich tales of the day narratives of strength, camaraderie, and the life-altering influence of artistic expression. He understood that the next day would bring a fresh start, another chance to keep crafting their shared story.

Like the embrace of a loving family, the warmth of his home welcomed him as he sought solace. Through their shared dreams and inexorable support, he discovered comfort and resilience. Lesedi understood that his artwork, though incomplete, was a testament to the collective masterpiece they were all crafting. It showcased the unwavering human spirit and the ability of art to shed light on the deepest recesses of the soul.

As the night grew darker, Lesedi struggled to find rest. His soul echoed with the experiences of the day and the incomplete masterpiece, igniting a yearning for closure. He felt the depth of his discovery, a source of inspiration that beckoned him to delve deeper.

Inspired by the spirit of adventure, Lesedi quietly left his room and headed towards the living room. The soft glow of moonlight filtered through the windows, creating a mesmerizing play of light and shadow on the walls. He got his sketchbook, opened it to a new page, and let his imagination take flight as he poured his thoughts onto the paper.

The pencil gracefully glided across the page, breathing life into the tales of the neighbours he had met earlier. Every brushstroke unveiled an intense courage, an unbreakable spirit, and an ability to find happiness in the face of hardship. Lesedi skillfully captured the essence of human experience, from the tender words of the elderly widow to the infectious laughter of the children, and the profound wisdom reflected in the eyes of the elderly man. In their shared experiences, he uncovered a tapestry of interwoven lives bonded by a common humanity.

As the night fell, Lesedi felt a deep feeling of gratitude for the meetings that had influenced his day. He came to see that his art was about more than just expressing himself, it was about creating a bigger story, a work of art that represented hope, harmony, and the resilience of the human spirit. With every stroke of his pencil, he rebelled against the despair that consumed their household and the surrounding society.

Sebokeng resembled a masterpiece yearning for its creator, revealed its vibrant colours as the sky observed with great attention. Lesedi stepped out of his modest dwelling, his worn sketchbook held firmly in his grasp. The aged pages seemed to hold the secrets of countless tales that danced within the limits of the small community.

Immersed in the loom of existence, Lesedi embraced each footfall. The bustling streets, filled with swirling dust and vibrant life, overflowed with diverse people. Just like the harmonious melodies that have echoed through the ages, the sound of children's laughter fills the air, creating a symphony of existence. Street vendors, with their colourful displays and tantalising treats, captivated the senses and sparked the imagination.

Lesedi, with the heart of an observer, immersed himself in the rich art of sights and sounds, allowing them to feel deeply within him. The resiliency that had been engraved into the wrinkled features of the old gave him hope for their immortal souls. The sparkling gaze of the youth, filled with uncharted aspirations, mirrored endless opportunities. Inspired by the great masters, Lesedi poured his heart and soul into these stories, infusing them with a vibrant energy through every line and stroke.

In the worn pages of his sketchbook, stories of triumph and hardship were quietly told. Lesedi beautifully captured the majestic curves of a mother, her eyes shining with undying love. He beautifully captured the dreams of a young boy, his eyes reflecting a world full of endless possibilities. Every stroke of his pencil, every splash of colour, revealed Sebokeng's undying spirit and the strength that coursed through its core.

Yet, in the midst of the vibrant tapestry, the dark hues of poverty and struggle intertwined their somber threads. The worn-out buildings stood as silent observers of the hardships that weighed on its residents. Whispers of struggle floated through the air, blending uneasily with the sounds of joy and merriment that filled the breeze.

Lesedi awoke with a feeling of excitement bubbling inside him, his sketchbook lying next to him on the well-worn mattress. Sebokeng's energy buzzed in the air, murmuring tales ready to be captured. As the sun began to rise, he embarked on his creative journey, navigating through the vibrant streets adorned with humble structures.

His initial subject appeared before him an aged gentleman with weathered features, each wrinkle telling a story of strength and perseverance.

Lesedi greeted him with a friendly smile. "Good morning, sir. May I take your picture, if that's alright with you?"

The old man's eyes gleamed with intrigue as he nodded in approval. Lesedi settled onto a wobbly stool, his pencil ready to make its mark on the page. As the sketch started to come together, he struck up a conversation with the elderly gentleman, captivated by his life story. The pencil glided over the page, capturing the man's physical appearance as well as the spirit of his experiences the obstacles, the achievements.

Inspired by the morning's triumph, Lesedi pressed on with his exploration of the township, capturing poignant scenes that deeply moved him. He came across a group of children engaged in a lively game of football in a dusty pitch. Their laughter filled the air, momentarily concealing the challenges they encountered on a daily basis. With his notebook out, Lesedi approached them and politely inquired, "Could I draw you all?" You have a contagious joy.

The children exchanged enthusiastic glances before eagerly gathering around him. During each sketch, he listened to their hopes and ambitions, which gave them the impression that they were being seen and heard. In spite of the challenges they faced, Lesedi's drawings were an attempt to capture their unwavering optimism.

As the day went on, Lesedi explored further into the township, his sketches growing more daring and filled with emotion. He came across a gathering of women, their colourful clothes sway-ing as they danced to the rhythm of their shared experiences.

Lesedi was captivated by the moment, his pencil effortlessly capturing the fluidity, elegance, and harmony they radiated.

In the midst of his artistic exploration, Lesedi found himself in a desolate alley where shadows moved with unrestrained freedom. It was then that he came face to face with the most significant adversary in his quest, which was poverty, taking the form of a little girl with sunken eyes and clothes that were in a state of disrepair. She leaned against a decaying wall, her eyes locked on an empty void.

Lesedi cautiously approached her, feeling the heaviness of her load. "Hello, would it be possible for me to sketch you?" he inquired, his voice filled with tenderness.

The girl's reply was a hushed murmur, barely discernible. "What is the reason behind your desire to draw me?" I feel like I am nothing.

Lesedi felt a pang in his heart, yet he stayed resolute. "Your story is worthy of being heard, of being witnessed."

As he started to draw, the girl's doubt gradually faded away, giving way to a flicker of a sense of hope. The pencil brought the page to life, capturing not just her physical appearance, but also the depth of her emotions. As they spoke, Lesedi discovered the hidden dreams that lay beneath the harsh realities of her life.

Through a collection of sketches, each captured the rich narratives of Sebokeng's residents. Lesedi's experiences painted a vibrant picture of victories, setbacks, aspirations, and determination, portraying a community characterised by its strength. It was in the middle of the colourful doodles that a feeling of togetherness and common humanity formed. His artwork had evolved into a mirror that reflected the challenges faced by the community, in addition to serving as a medium for personal expression. He thought that with every stroke of his pencil, he would be able to motivate others to make positive changes and ignite a spark of resiliency inside the hearts of those who saw his masterpieces.

He strolled through the lively streets of Sebokng, his sketchbook held firmly in his hands. The air was filled with a variety of scents: the enticing smell of freshly baked bread, the savoury aroma of braai meat, and the natural fragrance of the red soil that covered the pathways. Every stride he made appeared to effortlessly synchronise with the cadence of existence surrounding him.

Like a curious observer, Lesedi navigated through the bustling crowd, his eyes flitting from one face to another, in search of that elusive spark of inspiration. The people of Sebokeng bore stories etched into their expressions, their eyes brimming with aspirations, ambitions, and challenges. Lesedi longed to capture these stories on paper, to intertwine them in his sketches.

He discovered his place next to the lively market square, settling onto a wobbly wooden stool. The lively commotion of Sebokeng unfolded before him, resembling a captivating theatre production. His pencil moved gracefully across the pages of his sketchbook, expertly capturing the essence of every person who walked by. Lesedi's sketches capture the essence of life's fleeting moments the weathered face of an elderly woman, the purposeful steps of a young boy carrying water cans, the joyous laughter exchanged between friends. With each stroke of his pencil, Lesedi immortalises these scenes, ensuring they will never be forgotten.

Just as the sun reached its highest point in the sky, Lesedi decided to take a well-deserved break. He shut his eyes, experiencing the gentle heat on his face and the vibrant energy filling his ears. It was in this serene atmosphere that he unintentionally eavesdropped on a nearby conversation, picking up fragments of whispered voices filled with unease.

"Have you heard about the latest government initiative?" A man murmured softly, his words tinged with a blend of anticipation and hesitation. "Government initiative? What are they planning now?" a voice filled with doubt responded.

They have said that they would provide educational chances and possibilities for budding artists such as Lesedi. They have a burning desire to display our talent to the world.

Lesedi's heart raced with excitement, "Is it possible that this is true? Could I, with art, move beyond the limitations of my hometown?" He experienced a mixture of hope and scepticism, unsure of what to believe.

A shadow cast over his sketchbook and Lesedi looked up, locking eyes with a man standing in front of him. The stranger had a towering stature and a slender frame, with hands that bore the marks of time and were tinged with the remnants of artistic endeavors. His gaze possessed a profoundness that echoed the vastness of existence.

"You possess a remarkable talent, young artist," the stranger remarked, his voice tinged with an air of intrigue. "Your sketches have a depth that moves beyond what is visible. I've been watching you."

Lesedi's heart raced with a blend of wonder and intrigue. Who was this individual, and what were his intentions?

"I can show you a world beyond your wildest dreams," the stranger continued, his words lingering in the air like a masterpiece waiting to be unveiled. "However, it will demand absolute commitment, dedication, and a great desire to delve into the deep dimensions of your imagination."

Lesedi's mind was filled with a whirlwind of emotions, a blend of anticipation and nervousness. The stranger's offer had an irresistible allure, shrouded in an enigma air. Could he rely on this mysterious person? Could this be the opportunity to take his art to new levels?

"I... I want to learn," Lesedi stammered, his voice brimming with a resolute spirit. "I desire to venture into uncharted territories with my art."

The stranger's eyes sparkled with admiration, and a subtle grin played at the edges of his mouth. "Get ready, young artist, for a journey that will be truly different."

And just like that, the stranger vanished into the bustling crowd, leaving Lesedi with a blend of excitement and unease. Unbeknownst to him, his artistic journey was on the verge of a profound transformation. It would guide him towards a voyage of self-exploration, trials, and epiphanies that would not only influence his artwork but also redefine his sense of self.

Lesedi closed his sketchbook, his hands filled with anticipation. He embarked on a thrilling and uncertain journey, where his determination would be challenged, his creativity would be sparked, and the immense potential of his art would be unveiled.

* * *

As the sun began to rise and cast its golden glow across the sky, Lesedi's artwork was almost finished, capturing the tranquility of the early morning. He took a moment to appreciate the pages adorned with sketches and words, a beautiful reflection of the strength and interconnectedness of the human journey.

Lesedi embarked on a journey with a clear vision in mind.

He carefully gathered his artwork, brimming with passion and determination, and set off towards a local community center. He understood that his path as an artist was deeply connected to the community he aimed to inspire. Immersed in the stories of hope and resilience, he meticulously arranged his sketches on the walls of the centre, creating an exhibition that beckoned viewers to enter a world of inspiration.

News of Lesedi's artwork quickly spread, attracting a diverse range of individuals eager to witness his talent. Neighbours, friends, and strangers alike gathered in the space, deeply moved by the profound emotions expressed through his creations. Conversations ignited, hearts unfolded, and a shared energy of metamorphosis filled the room.

Lesedi stood among the crowd, his eyes gleaming with a blend of self-assurance and modesty. He witnessed the profound influence of his artwork, not only on the individuals depicted, but on the entire community. His incomplete masterpiece grew into a force that ignited change, serving as a powerful emblem of art's ability to mend, bring people together, and ignite creativity.

In that moment, Lesedi understood that his path as an artist was not limited to his home or his own goals. People connected with each other, worked together, and had a common goal of making the future better. He promised to keep drawing the stories of his community, giving people who don't have a voice a chance to be heard and putting light on things that haven't been seen.

Lesedi fully embraced his role as an artist and a catalyst for change, with his family always standing by his side, providing relentless support that fueled his strength. They set out on a shared voyage of healing and transformation, cultivating a glimmer of hope that blossomed into a world of endless possibilities for anyone touched by their art.

The unfinished artwork became a powerful representation of his unwavering determination. It served as a constant reminder that life, much like art, is an ongoing process of growth and evolution. Together, they saw their lives as a blank canvas, ready to be filled with the vibrant colours of their aspirations, transcending the limitations of their troubled past.

Lesedi's artwork captivated the community, filling him with a renewed sense of purpose. He delighted in the positive influence his creations had on others, as tales of strength and optimism spread throughout the community. Nevertheless, in the midst of this newfound joy, a formidable challenge loomed ahead, putting Lesedi's determination to the test.

One afternoon, as Lesedi returned from the community center, he found a letter waiting for him. The envelope was weathered, bearing no return address, and a sense of trepidation crept over him as he opened it. The letter revealed unexpected news that threatened to disrupt his newfound stability.

Lesedi's heart sank as he read the words filled with demands and bitterness. The weight of this revelation cast a shadow over the progress he had made. It seemed that even as his artwork had blossomed, the challenges of his past still held sway.

In the midst of a whirlwind of emotions, Lesedi found comfort in the embrace of his loved ones. He gathered his mother and Thabo, sharing the contents of the letter with them, just like a master storyteller unveiling a captivating tale. A sense of trepidation, frustration, and doubt permeated the room, as their shared aspirations faced an unexpected obstacle.

Thabo, a source of unwavering support, held Lesedi close, his words resonating with unrelenting resolve. "We will face this together, my little brother. We have faced numerous challenges in the past, and we refuse to allow this temporary setback to shape our future. Our art has the ability to rise above the deepest darkness."

Lesedi wholeheartedly dedicated himself to his craft, finding solace and introspection within the pages of his sketchbook. He expressed his inner struggles through his writing, searching for wisdom and understanding with every stroke of his pencil. Every line became a bold declaration against the obstacles that threatened to hinder his aspirations.

In the midst of this tempest, a guiding light appeared in the shape of Mpho, a seasoned neighbour renowned for her sagacity and fortitude. Upon hearing about Lesedi's challenge, she immediately made her way to his doorstep, her eyes brimming with empathy and understanding.

"Young Lesedi," she whispered gently, her voice filled with the wisdom of a lifetime, "I have seen the deep impact of your art. It has deeply resonated with people and sparked growth within our community. Don't let this setback overshadow your brilliance. Always keep in mind that obstacles can often be blessings in disguise."

Her words struck a chord with Lesedi, awakening a flicker of bravery in his tired soul. He came to understand that facing challenges was not a hindrance, but rather a driving force for personal development and change. Under Mpho's guidance, he discovered the power of his art to defy his stepfather's demands and bring attention to the widespread injustices in their community. Inspired by the same vision, Lesedi, Thabo, and Mpho came together to create a powerful alliance of strength. They tapped into their shared imagination to curate an art exhibition that shed light on the often unseen challenges experienced by numerous families. In their collective endeavours, their goal was to raise awareness, provide support, and ultimately, achieve justice for those impacted by the hardships of fractured families.

As the exhibition unfolded, Lesedi's artwork blossomed with a profound depth, capturing the raw emotions and resilience that emanated from his soul. Every brushstroke became a powerful statement of resistance against the obstacles that loomed over their aspirations, imbuing their art with an unrelenting strength that deeply touched all who beheld it.

On the day of the exhibition, the community flocked to the gallery, their presence, a powerful reminder of the impact of art and the strength of the human spirit. Lesedi's creations captured the essence of human experience, weaving tales of resilience and hope. Through his art, he encouraged viewers to contemplate their own paths and find strength in unity.

In the midst of the crowd, Lesedi noticed his stepfather, concealed in the darkness. But this time, Lesedi stood strong, his determination steadfast. He understood that his art had surpassed the expectations of any individual, transforming into a powerful emblem of resilience for those who had encountered comparable challenges.

As the night progressed, Lesedi and his family stood united, revelling in the overwhelming triumph of the exhibition. They had triumphed over the obstacle that loomed before them, displaying a remarkable strength of spirit. Lesedi discovered that his art possessed the ability to heal, inspire, and instigate change. It provided a platform for the marginalised and challenged the injustices that afflicted their community.

Inspired by the guidance of his loved ones and the unrelenting support of his community, Lesedi realised that his artistic journey held a greater purpose beyond his own ambitions. He dedicated his entire life to utilising his talent as a catalyst for change, illuminating even the most obscure areas and inspiring individuals to discover their inner resilience.

An old neighbour named Mpho had been a part of the neighbourhood for as long as anybody could remember, and she was renowned for her knowledge and resilience. Her kind demeanour and empathetic character had established her as a reliable source of comfort for those requiring assistance.

Mpho's life began in one of the townships of Soweto, where she faced numerous challenges. She came of age in a time of great turmoil when the nation was facing deep-seated racial injustice and political upheaval. These obstacles moulded her outlook and ignited her fervour for fairness and parity.

Even though she had personal losses and saw how hard things were for her community, Mpho became a symbol of hope. Her resolute commitment to creating an impact drove her to actively engage in grassroots movements and champion social change.

Through the course of her life, Mpho had amassed a vast amount of information and experience. Her modest attitude and compassionate character attracted individuals, who sought her wisdom and comfort in her words. She had a deep faith in the profound impact of storytelling and art, harnessing their potential to forge emotional connections and inspire meaningful transformation.

It was Mpho's personal experiences of being wronged and losing something that spurred her empathy for other people. She had a deep understanding of the pain that arises from fractured families and the profound impact it has on both individuals and communities. Inspired by the wisdom of great authors, she dedicated herself to helping others, offering support, direction, and useful suggestions.

Witnessing Lesedi's journey and learning of his stepfather's reappearance, Mpho couldn't help but acknowledge the profound significance of this moment. She recognised the immense difficulty Lesedi was up against, knowing it had the power to shatter his determination and hinder the strides he had taken. With a deep well of personal experiences to draw from, Mpho made a firm decision to be there for him, providing her valuable insights and steadfast encouragement.

Her presence in Lesedi's life brought a profound sense of stability and reassurance. Mpho's tireless belief in the revolutionary qualities of art and unwavering determination became a wellspring of motivation for Lesedi, propelling him onward in the face of adversity. As they spoke, she recounted tales of overcoming challenges, offering valuable insights that bolstered his determination.

In addition to her encounters with Lesedi and his family, Mpho broadened her participation in the neighbourhood to include other people. She was a renowned individual, providing assistance and encouragement to those seeking it. Her compassionate gestures, such as organising food drives and offering emotional support, won over the admiration of her neighbours. They admired her counsel, recognising the depth of wisdom and experience in her words.

Throughout her life, Mpho has experienced the profound impact of art, resilience, and the incredible strength that comes from a community standing together. She had a profound belief in the potential for personal growth that comes with every challenge, and she saw the indomitable spirit of humanity as capable of triumphing over any adversity.

Lesedi embarked on his artistic journey, facing the demands of his stepfather. Mpho, with her keen eye, recognised the immense potential of his art to bring about transformative change. With a profound understanding of the human condition, she was driven to help Lesedi harness his talent and illuminate the challenges experienced by fractured families, ultimately motivating others to discover their own strength.

Like a beacon of light, Mpho never ceased to inspire those around her, instilling a sense of hope in their hearts. Her steadfast dedication to justice, her deep compassion, and her faith in the strength of unity were a testament to the unstoppable determination of a woman who had devoted her life to creating positive change.

Chapter 3: The Power of Art

While Lesedi continued to pour his heart and soul into his artwork, he was located in the middle of the bustling township, where the beat of life surged through the neighbourhood streets. However, despite the fact that his unfinished work had become a symbol of resiliency, he continued to struggle with the burden of his stepfather's expectations and the constraints that poverty put on his aspirations throughout his life.

On a bright afternoon, while Lesedi was peacefully sitting in his front garden, capturing the essence of the people who strolled by, a beautiful melody filled the air. The melodic strumming of a guitar played with a captivating precision pierced through the bustling sounds of Sebokeng, captivating Lesedi's attention with an irresistible allure. He glanced upwards and noticed a small group of people gathered around a street performer, a well-known local musician named Thabo Molefe. Anyone lucky enough to be in the vicinity of Molefe could not help but be captivated by his mesmerising fingerwork on the strings and the weight of his story-filled voice.

Lesedi was captivated by the way Molefe's music effortlessly brought together the diverse elements of Sebokeng's life. The melodies captured stories of happiness, sadness, affection, and strength—the true essence of existence in Sebokeng. It felt as though the musician had discovered a method to express the silent emotions that permeated the atmosphere.

As Molefe's performance reached its peak, his gaze met Lesedi's, and a subtle smile appeared on his face. It seemed as though he had detected a connection with the young artist, a mutual comprehension of the immense potential that lies within the artistic spirit.

After the final note drifted away, Lesedi cautiously approached Molefe, feeling a rush of emotions swirling within him. The musician welcomed him with open arms, his gaze reflecting the profound experiences that shaped his existence.

"You have a talent," Molefe remarked, his voice carrying the soothing quality of a gentle breeze, "I could sense it in the way you observed my performance. Your sketches beautifully capture the true spirit of our township, much like my music aspires to do."

Lesedi, deeply moved by the musician's words, struggled to express his gratitude, "I appreciate it, sir. Your music... it has an enchanting quality. It has the power to unite people and evoke emotions within them."

"Art possesses the ability to surpass the limitations that society places upon us. It brings us together in our common humanity and serves as a reminder that we all have stories to share, each one distinct and special," Molefe nodded in affirmation.

Just like Lesedi, Molefe's presence had a profound impact on him, causing a significant transformation. As time went on, the musician not only became a mentor to Lesedi, but also a close friend, providing guidance and support on his artistic journey. Molefe saw a connection with Lesedi and was committed to sharing more than just technical knowledge. He wanted to teach the young artist valuable life lessons that would influence their worldview. Molefe's unwavering faith in Lesedi's abilities shone brightly, guiding the way towards a future filled with immense possibilities.

Lesedi and Molefe frequently found themselves in deep conversation, exchanging tales of their experiences and the challenges they had encountered. Molefe shared his personal journey, recounting a time when he faced the challenges of being an artist, dealing with rejection and financial difficulties. He shared with Lesedi about the numerous instances when he had questioned his own talent and purpose.

"Struggles, my young friend," Molefe would add, "are not obstacles, they are opportunities—because every challenge is a chance to grow. They serve as the foundation for the masterpieces we craft. It is through our pain, doubts, and challenges that we discover the deepest wellspring of inspiration."

Leaning back in his chair, a distant gaze in his eyes, "you know, Lesedi, my journey has not always been without obstacles. There were moments when I doubted my abilities as an artist and wondered if my work would ever be appreciated."

Lesedi, full of curiosity, enquired. "Oh, come on, Molefe! Your music possesses an enchanting quality. It resonates with individuals on a profound level."

Molefe smiling knowingly, "Ah, my young friend, that's the magic of art. It has the ability to make your worries into something truly remarkable. The melodies you hear now were crafted through extensive dedication, facing setbacks, and questioning oneself."

Lesedi eagerly engaged, "So, what inspired you to persevere, man? How did you discover the inner resolve to conquer those uncertainties?"

Reflecting on the situation, Molefe said, "My young friend, difficulties are not impediments, rather, they are opportunities. They serve as the foundation for the masterpieces we craft. Just as a great author once wrote, 'In the midst of our suffering, our uncertainties, and the difficulties we face, we discover the most deep sources of inspiration.'"

"I think I'm starting to see that now," Lesedi said, nodding his head in response.

"Maybe the challenges of this area and my stepfather's demands aren't obstacles at all, but rather sources of inspiration. As you put it, Lesedi, it is exactly what I mean. Let that fire burn brightly as you create a work of art that will move and inspire those going through tough times. Pain may be turned into beauty through your creativity."

In a moment of inspiration, Lesedi said, "I will, Molefe. All of it will be channelled into my art, and I will let each stroke of my pencil to be a relief and a method to communicate what words are unable to describe."

"That's the spirit, my young friend," Molefe said as he placed his hand on Lesedi's shoulder. "Face the difficulties head-on; that's when your creativity will really shine. Also, keep in mind that you are not travelling alone on this path. We're all on this journey together, gaining wisdom from one another as we go."

Their conversation stretched well into the night, as Lesedi soaked up not just technical knowledge, but also the deep wisdom of art and resilience that Molefe shared.

Lesedi's artistic journey took a significant turn, as he began to see his challenges as opportunities for growth, much like Molefe had done in the past.

Lesedi soaked up these words with eagerness, recognising that his stepfather's expectations and the challenges of his hometown were not obstacles, but rather inspiration for his creativity.

Under Molefe's guidance, he would discover a way to express his emotions through his artworks, using each stroke of his pencils and paints as a form of catharsis.

Molefe also mentored Lesedi in the practical aspects of the art world, broadening Lesedi's horizons beyond the boundaries of his small township. Molefe understood that Lesedi needed more than just artistic talent to overcome the challenges of their circumstances. He had a deep appreciation for the value of hands-on experience and immersing oneself in the vast realm of art.

Molefe guided Lesedi in navigating the practical aspects of the art industry, imparting valuable knowledge on marketing his work and achieving financial stability as an artist. They dedicated countless hours to exploring the significance of pre-sentation, mastering the art of capturing his artwork through photography, and honing their skills in crafting captivating artist statements. Molefe highlighted the importance of art as a means of communication, emphasising that Lesedi's presentation of his work played a vital role in expressing its profound depth and significance.

Molefe was determined to go beyond just teaching Lesedi theoretical knowledge, he strongly believed in the importance of practical learning. To help Lesedi master the practical aspects of the art world, he guided him through the complexities of art marketing and presentation.

* * *

On a bright morning, Molefe guided Lesedi to a quaint photography studio nestled in the bustling city. They encountered a seasoned photographer with a knack for capturing artwork.

Molefe emphasised the importance of using high-quality images to effectively market art and introduced Lesedi to Samuel, a friendly photographer. Samuel, with his vast experience working alongside various artists, patiently mentored Lesedi in the art of capturing his artwork with precision. He showed how to expertly utilise high-quality cameras and lighting gear to capture the intricate details, textures, and colours in Lesedi's artwork. Molefe highlighted the importance of using high-quality images to not only capture the attention of potential buyers but also to effectively communicate the depth and significance of the artwork.

As Lesedi captured images of his intricate sketches and paintings, he came to appreciate the significance of meticulousness and a keen eye for detail. Samuel taught him valuable techniques to eliminate glare, achieve precise colour reproduction, and uphold consistency throughout his portfolio. Lesedi had a profound experience, discovering that the art-making process goes far beyond the confines of a sketchbook or canvas and delves into the realm of visual representation.

After their photography session, Molefe brought Lesedi to a graphic design studio. Here, they encountered a skilled graphic designer named Emma, who had a knack for crafting captivating artist statements and promotional materials. Molefe emphasised the importance of effective and captivating communication when showcasing one's work to potential buyers and galleries.

With Emma's guidance, Molefe mastered the skill of crafting artist statements that beautifully captured the essence of his creative process and effectively conveyed the emotional and conceptual dimensions of his art. Emma urged him to incorporate personal anecdotes and the stories behind his sketches into his statements.

She emphasised that these narratives would enable viewers to establish a profound connection with his work.

Molefe, inspired by Lesedi's passion for learning, also accompanied him on visits to local galleries and exhibitions. They examined the ways in which different artists showcased their work, carefully considering the framing choices, lighting design, and wall arrangements. Molefe emphasised the importance of how an artwork is displayed, as it can greatly influence the viewer's perception and emotional connection.

Lesedi soon came to understand that presentation held a significance beyond being a mere formality; it was a vital component of the artistic journey. He discovered the importance of effectively marketing his work and establishing a compelling visual identity to distinguish himself in the fiercely competitive art world.

Now that Lesedi had this fresh information, he started putting it to use. He made sure to invest in top-notch photography equipment to capture his artwork with utmost precision. He skilfully composed artist statements that intertwined the stories of his sketches and paintings. And just like an artist who is deeply passionate about his craft, he took great care in how he showcased his work, making sure that those who experienced it could truly lose themselves in the captivating narratives woven into each piece.

Molefe's mentorship, combined with his practical expertise, gave Lesedi the confidence to navigate the intricacies of the art industry. He possessed a unique ability to not only create art, but also to effectively communicate his profound passion and the unwavering strength of his community.

***

On a sunny Saturday morning, Molefe brought Lesedi to a charming art studio in the heart of the city, where a vibrant community of artists gathered. Lesedi's eyes filled with wonder as they neared the vibrant mural that graced the outer wall. It captured the essence of the artistic community, highlighting the energy and excitement that lay ahead. The studio exuded an atmosphere of boundless creativity, with its walls adorned with an exquisite collection of paintings, sculptures, and mixed-media pieces.

Upon entering, Lesedi was overcome with a profound sense of belonging that he had never encountered previously. The artists welcomed him with open arms and genuine excitement, ready to embrace a new addition to their creative community.

The walls were filled with a mesmerising array of paintings, ranging from vibrant landscapes that exuded vitality to abstract pieces that invited contemplation. Works of art in different sizes stood proudly, each with its own unique tale to tell, while innovative mixed-media pieces stretched the limits of the mind's eye.

The ambiance inside was vibrant, pulsating with the artistic fervour of the individuals who congregated there. Lesedi was surrounded by the intoxicating aroma of acrylic paint, which mingled harmoniously with the soft murmur of conversation, creating a captivating sensory experience. He experienced the sensation of being a wanderer who had fortuitously discovered a captivating oasis.

The artists, a diverse and passionate group, were quick to spot the newcomers. Their faces were filled with warmth and genuine excitement as they approached Lesedi and Molefe. It was a warm and inclusive gathering, a true reflection of the close-knit and encouraging nature of this creative community.

Lesedi's sketchbook and portfolio captured everyone's gaze. Artists gathered around, studying his work with a blend of curiosity and attentiveness. His talent and the raw emotion evident in his sketches and paintings were highly praised. But what made this community unique was their eagerness to offer helpful feedback.

Every artist contributed their own distinct viewpoint to the discussion. Some techniques were suggested to enhance the depth of shading, while others provided insights into colour theory and composition. Lesedi embraced their feedback with a receptive mindset, recognising that this spirit of collaboration was a driving force for personal development.

The artists also discussed their personal journeys in the art market, recounting the thrill of their initial exhibitions and the difficulties they faced in determining the right prices for their artwork. They emphasised the significance of establishing connections with galleries, art collectors, and fellow artists. Lesedi listened attentively, fully aware of the immense value this knowledge held for his journey.

As the day progressed, Lesedi discovered himself immersed in a wealth of wisdom and motivation. The artists were not just mentors, but also kindred spirits who had unwavering faith in his potential. They highlighted the importance of art as a collective expression of creativity, emphasising its power to bring people together.

Lesedi departed from the art studio that day with a newfound determination. He had discovered his tribe, a group of artists who would stand by him as he pursued his goal of creating a significant impact with his art.

He had acquired a wealth of knowledge, formed meaningful connections, and was filled with boundless inspiration that would profoundly influence his artistic path in the years ahead.

His sketchbook and portfolio were carefully examined, sparking curiosity. The artists admired his talent and offered valuable feedback to help him improve his technique.

They generously shared their personal experiences of entering the art market and provided valuable advice on pricing, exhibiting, and networking. Lesedi eagerly devoured the wealth of knowledge.

Still, Lesedi was filled with conflicting emotions.

Just as the demands of his stepfather continued to hang over him, the burden of poverty remained a constant weight on his shoulders. He grappled with the conflict between his artistic dreams and the seemingly insurmountable practical obstacles.

One evening, as he sat alone in his room, the soft glow of a single candle dancing, Lesedi faced his inner turmoil. Uncertainty consumed him, ready to extinguish the spark of his aspirations.

As Lesedi sits in his chamber, the shifting shadows generated by the flickering candle make him wonder, "Is this truly something I can handle? Is it possible to rise above the limitations of this space, the burden of our hardships?"

"Lesedi, you're a dreamer," said Doubt in a low voice. "Dreams alone cannot provide for your family or cover your expenses."

The voice of Lesedi was barely audible above a whisper as he hesitated before continuing, "But art... it's more than just dreams. It's a method of sharing our narratives, amplifying the voices of those who have been silenced."

Doubt said sarcastically, "Oh, because stories are just so practical and useful, right?"

As he closes his eyes and recalls, Lesedi said, "My young friend, difficulties are not impediments; rather, they are opportunities. They serve as the foundation for the masterpieces we craft. We discover the deepest sources of inspiration in the midst of our suffering, uncertainties, and difficulties."

As Lesedi said, "I can't let you put out this flame. Molefe said something that is very true. Art possesses the power to bring people together, ignite inspiration, and create meaningful changes. It's not only about myself, it's about all of us, our community."

Doubt receded, "But how can you get around the difficulties that are encountered in everyday life?"

"One step at a time." As promised, Lesedi said. "I aspire to learn, evolve, and utilise my artistic abilities to illuminate the shadows that envelop our world. In the face of adversity, my spirit remains unyielding, refusing to be crushed by the weight of poverty."

During that quiet moment, Lesedi made a personal promise to himself. He would persistently follow his artistic aspirations, not in spite of the difficulties, but rather as a result of those difficulties. His passion blazed fiercely, dispelling any doubts that had loomed over it. Inspired by the wisdom of Molefe and the resilience of his community, he would channel his artistic talents to shape a brighter future for everyone.

After recommitting himself, Lesedi made a serious vow to himself. He would use his art to not only break free from the things that held him back, but also to bring attention to the wrongs that were happening in his community. His work would inspire change, provide a platform to the marginalised, and prove that the human spirit can overcome adversity.

***

Deep into the night, Lesedi painstakingly captured the portraits of those who had endured the trials of destitution and hardship by his side. Despite the hard reality that they were confronted with, his pencil danced over the paper, etching the lines of their stories, the strength that was seen in their eyes, and the hopes that had refused to die under the pressure. As he continued to draw, he had a tremendous feeling of purpose that extended beyond the bounds of his notebook. He felt a greater connection to his origins with each stroke.

His sketches wouldn't just be pictures; they would speak for those who couldn't, sharing stories of strength, hope, and the unwavering human spirit. His work, he believed, should serve as a reflection of his community's trials and tribulations, a tribute to their resilience.

Lesedi understood the urgent need to bring attention to the injustices that afflicted his community. The poverty, lack of opportunities, and systemic inequalities that they faced were in dire need of being exposed. He embraced the idea that art possessed the ability to evoke empathy, ignite discussions, and inspire transformative action.

Working tirelessly into the night, Lesedi felt a deep sense of responsibility. His sketches were more than just simple lines on paper; they had the power to inspire action. He sought to push boundaries, challenge norms, and ignite a spark of inspiration in those who beheld his portraits.

The next day, Lesedi shared his vision with Molefe, who smiled proudly and nodded in agreement. Molefe realised that Lesedi had set out on a journey that reached far beyond the boundaries of the township. He had become an artist driven by a mission, a storyteller fuelled by a purpose, and a symbol of hope for those who had once felt their voices would never be heard.

Lesedi's unwavering commitment to using his art to make a difference in society would guide him through a journey marked by obstacles and victories. However, he had transcended any restrictions and was driven by an intense desire to create an impact. His drawings would serve as the blueprint for change, illuminating his neighborhood's future with each stroke.

Lesedi's work evolved and grew with each passing day, transforming into something truly extraordinary. It was like a mirror that showed the beauty and problems of the neighbourhood. It reignited hope in those who had lost it and became a powerful force for change, breaking through poverty and hardship.

Molefe urged Lesedi to take part in local art exhibitions and galleries, recognising the importance of exposing his talent to a wider audience for his artistic development. Lesedi hesitated initially, questioning whether his work would have a lasting impact beyond the township. Molefe's steadfast faith in him inspired him to take a leap of faith.

His journey took on a greater purpose, as he sought to illuminate the challenges and victories of others through his talent. Lesedi was becoming a source of inspiration, not only for himself but for his entire community, demonstrating the transformative power of art and its ability to create positive change.

This was his second group exhibition, and it was an anxiety-inducing experience for him. Hee observed with pride that a diverse range of individuals, from art aficionados to collectors, carefully studied his collection of framed sketches. The intense emotion and captivating narrative in his works resonated deeply with the audience. His artworks vividly portrayed the struggles, hope, and resilience of Sebokeng, capturing the essence of its spirit.

News of Lesedi's talent quickly spread far and wide. His work was not only admired but also celebrated. Local newspapers highlighted the young artist's ability to illuminate the human experience in Sebokeng through his talent. His works began to gain popularity, attracting not only investors but also individuals who resonated with the narratives conveyed through his art.

Under Molefe's guidance, Lesedi began to generate income from his artistic endeavours. He was able to sell his sketches and paintings, and soon enough, he started receiving numerous commissions. It was a pivotal moment in his life, as he came to the realisation that his love and dedication could also bring financial security to his family.

However, even with his increasing achievements, Lesedi maintained a humble attitude. He reflected on the challenges that had led him to this moment and the unwavering backing of his loved ones, particularly his mother and Thabo.

Lesedi and Molefe joined forces on a project that aimed to foster unity within their community, as Lesedi's artistic journey continued to thrive. They hosted a mural-painting event, extending an invitation to township residents to participate in a grand artwork that honoured the values of togetherness and strength. It was a clear demonstration of how art can bring people together and inspire transformation.

Like a wise sage, Molefe not only imparted his knowledge of art to Lesedi, but also instilled in him a deep conviction in the life-changing potential of creativity. Lesedi had developed a unique perspective, perceiving the world with the keen eye of an artist. He had a knack for finding inspiration in the most unexpected corners and channelling his creative abilities towards positive endeavours.

The more Lesedi's art developed, the more he saw that his path was about more than simply making it big, it was also about leaving his community with a legacy of strength and optimism. Thanks to Molefe's encouragement and a strong network of other artists, Lesedi was making great strides towards his goal of making a good impact on Sebokeng which had moulded him through his art.

Chapter 4: Brushstrokes of Hope

It was a melancholic afternoon, the sky filled with dark clouds heavy with unshed tears. Lesedi found solace in his small, makeshift studio, where the bustling sounds of Sebokeng life faded into the background, leaving him alone with his thoughts.

His easel stood before him, displaying a half-finished canvas that seemed to ridicule his every effort. The room overflowed with the remnants of his past creations, sketches and paintings that once captured the spirit of his lively community. Now, they seemed to embody echoes of his previous inspiration.

As Lesedi's artistic journey unfolded, he found himself grappling with a storm of uncertainty. Once, his passion burned fiercely, but now it flickered weakly, struggling against the force of adversity. Just as dreams can be a wellspring of motivation, they can also become an overwhelming weight that weighs heavily on one's shoulders.

His sketches lacked the vitality and emotional depth that once defined them, appearing more like superficial marks on a page. The once vibrant tales had lost their essence, reduced to mere markings on a lifeless sheet. Uncertainty slithered into his thoughts, whispering its toxic words that dampened his creative spirit.

Lesedi would carefully examine his work, every brushstroke or pencil line becoming a mirror of his doubts. He wondered if his talent was just a mirage, if he could truly harness art as a catalyst for transformation. The vivid colours that had once emanated from his spirit now appeared dull, as if the vitality had been sapped from them by the world.

Every time he opened his sketchbook, a sense of insufficiency washed over him. It felt as if his creative inspiration had deserted him, leaving him stranded in a desolate artistic realm. He felt overwhelmed by the path he had chosen, his doubts growing stronger with every stroke of his pencil.

"What's the point?" he would murmur to himself, his gaze fixed on a half-finished sketch. "Do these lines and colours hold the power to truly bring about change? Can my art have an impact in a world where hope is a rare commodity? Is it enough?"

His inner struggle reverberated in the stillness of his room as he whispered to himself, his voice tinged with uncertainty. He stared at the incomplete sketch on his desk, feeling as though the lines and colours were silently judging him. They appeared to question him, wondering if his art could truly have an impact in a place where hope was scarce, like water in a desert.

He reclined in his seat, energetically running his fingers through his abundant locks as if attempting to physically rid of the uncertainty. The atmosphere in the room was suffocating as if the walls were slowly constricting around him. Outside, Sebokeng carried on with its daily affairs, a realm where hardship was a regular occurrence, where aspirations often faded away before they could take root.

"What's the point?" he exclaimed, his voice growing louder as if he was searching for an answer that outweighed the limits of his mind.

The question hung in the air, unspoken yet tangible. It was a question that had troubled artists and dreamers for centuries, and Lesedi now wrestled with it.

Kgalalelo entered the room with a gentle demeanour, her eyes immediately catching Lesedi's distress. "Lesedi, my dear, what seems to be troubling you?" she asked softly.

Lesedi gazes upwards, his eyes welling with tears of frustration. "Mama, I'm unsure if I can continue on this path. My art... it lacks meaning. I feel a sense of emptiness within me."

"Every artist goes through moments like this, my son," she said as she moved closer to him and placed a reassuring hand on his shoulder. "It's a necessary step on the path. It's not only about having flawless lines or brilliant colours in your artwork, Lesedi. Not only is it about your heart and soul but also about the stories you share with people."

Lesedi takes a deep breath, gazing at his mother with a sense of uncertainty. "What if I've lost it? What if I can't find my way back?" he wonders aloud.

Lesedi's mother smiled gently, "You still have it, Lesedi. You still have it within you. Just as life's challenges test us, we must weather the storm to witness the beauty that lies beyond.

Continue to express yourself through your art and storytelling. You hold the power to deeply connect with others, igniting inspiration and instilling a sense of hope."

He pondered the expressions on the faces of the individuals in his community—their challenges, their difficulties, their tireless strength. Could his artistic creations truly act as a guiding light, a wellspring of motivation, in a location where desolation frequently prevailed? Would the strokes and hues on his sketchbook sheets be sufficient to counter the prevailing gloom that bound them?

Lesedi's gaze wandered to the walls of his room, graced with his own artwork. Each piece held a story, a fragment of Sebokeng's essence. However, in this moment of uncertainty, their significance seemed to fade.

The art that had once been a testament to his fervour now appeared as mere embellishments, feeble endeavours to encapsulate the unbreakable spirit of the community.

Lesedi found himself grappling with the immense pressure of his own dreams and the expectations of others. He questioned whether he had set his goals impossibly high, and whether his dreams were mere figments of his imagination. The nagging doubts suggested that he may not possess the necessary talent for his chosen path, and that his artistic endeavours held little significance in the larger loom of life. As Lesedi embarked on his artistic journey, the weight of expectations grew heavier with each step. The once-promising path to his dreams now appeared obscured by doubt. His personal ambitions, driven by the need to prove himself and uplift his family from poverty, hovered over him like an unstoppable tempest. As he worked late into the night, bent over his sketchbook, uncertainties began to seep in like shadows. The burden of his own lofty goals murmured that perhaps he had set the bar too high. The aspirations that had once served as guiding lights now appeared far away, mere fleeting glimpses in the vast expanse of an unpredictable horizon.

Sighed deeply, his hand shaking slightly as he tried to sketch "Why does it feel so hard now? Why do these lines no longer flow like they used to?"

Muttered to himself, frustration clear in his voice "Maybe I'm not cut out for this. Maybe I've been fooling myself all along."

His hand moved tentatively across the canvas, uncertainty seeping in with every stroke. "You're aiming too high."

The voice of Doubt whispered like a persistent shadow. "Can your art really bring about change and hope? Are you not just lying to yourself and just seeking mere illusions?"

Lesedi hesitated, feeling the heaviness of uncertainty fill the room like a suffocating mist. The pencil hovered uncertainly above the canvas, the once-vibrant vision now clouded by the negative murmurs that reverberated in his thoughts.

"What if your dreams are simply illusions?" The way to Doubt persisted, entwining itself within the very essence of his creativity. "In a world where hope is a rare commodity, do you truly have faith in the power of your sketches to ignite change? You're just another dreamer in a world that can often be discouraging."

His shoulders sagged beneath the burden of pessimism.

Every brushstroke, once filled with intention, now felt like a meandering journey through a realm of uncertainty. The vibrant colors that used to dance with vitality on his canvas now appeared subdued, as if their brilliance had been sapped by the unyielding doubt.

"Look around you," the Doubt persisted, its voice growing

sharper. "Your community is overwhelmed with challenges. Your sketches won't make a difference. You're not a saviour; you're just an artist with ambitious visions that will not come to fruition."

In the room, where creativity once flourished, now resounded the mocking whispers of doubt. Lesedi grappled with the negative story that loomed over his ambitions.

The conflict between his yearning to make a difference and the nagging belief that his endeavours were in vain became an unspoken war, fought brushstroke by brushstroke on the canvas of his aspirations.

In the depths of his thoughts, Lesedi grappled with insecurities that threatened to overshadow the vivid hues of his dreams. He pondered if his artistic pursuits were mere illusions, as self-doubt insinuated that he may not possess the innate talent he envisioned for his art.

His brush danced across the canvas, crafting a tale of the challenges woven into the tapestry of his community.

Yet, amidst each stroke, a shadow of uncertainty crept in.

"Who will care about these images?" It taunted, its voice insidious. "Are you not merely contributing to a vast sea of troubles?"

Lesedi experienced the heaviness of every word as if they were dragging down the momentum of his creativity. The once vivid scenes of endurance he aimed to portray now appeared insignificant, overshadowed by the nagging uncertainty that reverberated within him.

"Your art won't have any impact," the Doubt persisted, its voice becoming more prominent. "These images, they won't bring about any change. You're just one voice among many in a sea of larger issues. What kind of impact can your sketches really make?"

His brushstrokes took on a contemplative quality, as if searching for deeper meaning. The vibrant colours he once used now took on a more subdued tone, reflecting the doubts that lingered in his mind. Lesedi wrestled with the idea that his art, intended to inspire and uplift, could potentially be overshadowed by the multitude of obstacles that lay before him.

"Look at the bigger picture," the doubt scoffed, its tone dripping with cynicism. "Your sketches won't make a difference in society's trajectory. You're not a catalyst for change; you're just an artist with idealistic desires."

In the midst of his community's struggles, Lesedi confronted the uncertainty that threatened to overshadow the meaning behind his creations. The conflict between his aspiration to make a difference and the doubt that questioned the influence of his art became a silent battle, fought within the realm of his dreams. Lesedi found himself at the centre of a contradiction.

On one hand, he passionately pursued his dreams, each brushstroke and line on the canvas a testament to his tireless dedication. Yet, on the other hand, he grappled with the fear that these dreams might never become reality. As he journeyed through the maze of uncertainty and fixed resolve, Lesedi pondered the possibility of his dreams. The turmoil inside him mirrored the obstacles he faced externally—poverty, family conflicts, and the constant fear of his stepfather's volatile nature.

The dreams that once soared like kites in a clear sky now appeared to be caught in the unpredictable winds of reality. Lesedi's efforts to elevate his art to new heights were constantly challenged by the shadows of uncertainty, which made him question the feasibility of his endeavours. Each artistic pursuit became a delicate balance between hope and despair, with the constant presence of self-doubt lurking beneath.

He struggled with the dilemma of desiring to make an impact with his art, yet being afraid that the enormity of the challenges around him could make his endeavours pointless. The painting became a battlefield where the vibrant hues of optimism clashed with the murky shades of uncertainty, and Lesedi, the artist, found himself at the crossroads of inspiration and doubt.

Imprisoned within the walls of his own home, Lesedi bore the burden of his stepfather's relentless expectations and the torment of emotional mistreatment, as if they were unbreakable chains binding him to a life he yearned to escape. Lesedi's stepfather, trapped in the clutches of alcohol, became a symbol of chaos in their home.

His mere presence enveloped their lives in darkness, suffocating the very essence of their existence. His emotions were as unpredictable as the wind, swinging between shallow apologies that held a glimmer of sincerity, only to be quickly replaced by uncontrollable fits of rage.

The impact of his stepfather's words and actions had the ability to completely undermine Lesedi's self-assurance. In the aftermath of his outbursts, Lesedi frequently found himself doubting his own value and aspirations. The tumultuous emotional atmosphere within their household gradually eroded the bedrock of his self-confidence, leaving him feeling uncertain and unsteady.

Like a gripping novel character, the man in question possessed an enigmatic nature that left those around him on edge. The emotional rollercoaster seemed never-ending, with hurtful words leaving a lasting impact on Lesedi's sensitive heart and artistic spirit.

* * *

It was an intense evening in the household. Lesedi sat at the table, his sketchbook open but forgotten, as his stepfather's unpredictable moods created an atmosphere of uncertainty. His stepfather's anger was like an impending storm, brewing and ready to disrupt the delicate tranquility.

Lesedi murmured to himself, "Here we go again..."

Lesedi's stepfather speaks incoherently, his mood is as un-predictable as ever.

Stepfather frustrated, "What's this, young one? Always lost in your thoughts and creating. Do you believe you're better than us? Your artistic pursuits will not provide sustenance!"

Lesedi hangs his head, his confidence fading as he absorbs the impact of his stepfather's words.

Whispering gently to himself, "I am going to achieve personal goals and help my family..."

Chuckling cynically he said, "Assisting the family? Your mother and brother require someone who can truly step up, not just a dreamer who struggles to provide."

The atmosphere in the room is charged with intense emotions. Lesedi's stepfather oscillates between bursts of anger and fleet-ing moments of regret, creating a constant cycle of emotional turmoil.

Lesedi's heart aches as his stepfather's anger lingers, his words piercing like sharp blades.

Stepfather leaning in, his breath smelling strongly of alcohol,

"Don't expect your art to cover your expenses, young man. Avoid getting too absorbed in your imaginative world of colours and lines."

Lesedi feels a heavy weight on his chest, suffocating under the weight of the oppressive atmosphere. The dreams that once filled him with hope now appear delicate and fleeting, overshadowed by the harsh reality imposed by his stepfather.

The atmosphere in the room is heavy with tension, leaving Lesedi's creative spirit feeling deflated as if his artistic sanctuary has lost its vitality.

Lesedi inhales deeply, his voice quivering yet determined. "I want to leave a lasting impact, to show that life holds greater meaning."

The gaze of his stepfather narrows, filled with a dismissive disdain, "Do you really still believe that your art has the power to make a difference in the world? Keep dreaming, my boy. The reality is that you will find yourself facing the same challenges and feeling isolated, just like me."

Lesedi's self-assurance falters after the impact of his stepfather's hurtful words takes hold.

Whispering to himself, "I refuse to succumb to this fate. I will not allow the shadows to consume me."

The stepfather's voice, reminiscent of a weathered soul, carried a hint of melancholy and reflection as he embarked on the tale of his personal hardships.

Laughs bitterly, "You know, Lesedi, I once had dreams as well. I ventured into the world of entrepreneurship, opening a humble tavern, with hopes of bringing abundance to my family. However, fate had other plans. The weight of taxes, debts, and fierce competition swiftly dismantled my dreams. It seems that life has a knack for extinguishing one's dreams, regardless of the effort put forth."

Lesedi listened intently, his heart heavy with a profound sense of melancholy. The man's story served as a poignant testament to the delicate nature of dreams when confronted with the unforgiving truths of the world.

Stepfather's voice laden with weight, "I had high hopes for my future, but unfortunately, it all turned out to be in vain. It left me feeling utterly let down. It's important, Lesedi, not to let your dreams cloud your judgment. The reality is that the world tends to be indifferent towards those who dare to dream. "

As the stepfather spoke, a heavy cloud of despair filled the room. It stood in stark contrast to Lesedi's resolute resolve. The lingering presence of past mistakes and missed opportunities cast a shadow, serving as a constant reminder of the challenges that have the potential to shape one's existence.

Lesedi said gently, "I understand your perspective, but I refuse to let projected fear dictate my actions. I am determined to take a leap of faith and strive to achieve my full potential."

In the midst of the tense atmosphere, the stepfather's face remained impassive, showing no support for Lesedi's aspirations. The room was enveloped in an unsettling quiet as if it housed a clash between two contrasting realms - one bursting with youthful dreams, the other burdened by the weight of past mistakes.

Lesedi's artistic dreams appear as ethereal as a mirage, overshadowed by the weight of his stepfather's volatile temper, empty words, and inebriated criticism. Yet, amidst the darkness, a faint ember of determination continues to burn within him. In the midst of the heavy atmosphere, Lesedi, overwhelmed by a surge of frustration and powerlessness, decides to shut his sketchbook, unwilling to expose his art to such a toxic environment.

In the aftermath, a feeling of hopelessness engulfed him, casting a sombre atmosphere. The erratic behaviour of his stepfather loomed over him, dampening his ambitions and stifling the vitality of his creative visions.

The heaviness of his stepfather's scornful remarks hung in the air, suffocating Lesedi with a sense of powerlessness, as if he were merely an observer in his own existence, stripped of the ability to chase his dreams.

Lesedi's aspirations to become an artist and shed light on the challenges faced by his community appeared to fade as his stepfather's harsh comments continued. These words acted as a stifling force, restricting his imagination and limiting his sense of what was achievable.

After his stepfather stumbles away, Lesedi pauses to collect his thoughts, safeguarding his creative spirit from the toxic atmosphere that had filled the room. Though his sanctuary feels tainted, a faint spark of optimism flickers in his eyes, as he silently nurtures a resolve to prove his stepfather's doubts unfounded.

Living in a tumultuous household, Lesedi found himself drained by the rollercoaster of emotions. The lack of stability and support hindered his growth and well-being.

Each day became a battle against the unpredictable, with his stepfather's hurtful words weighing heavily on him, casting a shadow over his once vibrant dreams.

His art, once a symbol of his dreams, now seemed tainted by the negativity that filled their home. The refuge he once found in his sketches was now overshadowed by the toxic atmosphere, making it harder for him to find solace and inspiration in his work.

Similar to the tempestuous thunderstorms that ravaged the township, Lesedi found himself burdened with the weight of his mentally ill uncle's erratic behaviour and unpredictable outbursts.

It was yet another challenge he had to face and overcome.

Lesedi's uncle, grappling with mental illness, served as a constant reminder of the arbitrary behaviour of life in the township. His actions were a turbulent mix of ups and downs, and his emotional outbursts resembled bolts of lightning capable of shattering the delicate tranquility of their household.

On certain days, his uncle would become immersed in the depths of his own thoughts, appearing distant and confused, communicating in enigmatic language that only he could understand. On other occasions, he would burst into episodes of intense rage and exasperation, yelling at invisible foes or even at the entire world.

For Lesedi, experiencing these episodes felt like teetering on the brink of a deep abyss, never knowing when the ground might crumble beneath him. The perpetual uncertainty weighed heavily on his mind, burdening his spirit and making it challenging to concentrate on his art.

As an artist, Lesedi was deeply compelled to express himself and share the stories of his community through his work. However, the disorder and disarray within his home seemed to mirror the inner turmoil he experienced. His uncle's unpredictable behaviour seemed to reflect the doubts and fears that loomed over him, threatening to engulf him completely.

In the midst of a tumultuous environment, Lesedi found himself grappling with the clash between his stepfather's unpredictability and his uncle's mental health struggles. This created a pervasive tension that made it increasingly difficult for him to find solace or inspiration in his art. The weight of his uncle's distress, coupled with his own sense of helplessness, only added to the overwhelming atmosphere.

It was as if Lesedi was trapped in the centre of a storm, unable to bring any calm to the chaos that surrounded him. He had once hoped that his home would be a sanctuary, a place where he could escape the harsh realities of the township. Unfortunately, it had transformed into a battlefield where words and emotional wounds were the weapons of choice.

Instead of providing comfort, his home became a breeding ground for self-doubt.

In these moments, Lesedi felt as if his internal struggles and the chaotic ambiance of his surroundings were intertwined, creating a turbulent canvas that tested his artistic abilities.

In his home, a powerful force of negative energy loomed.

It carried the echoes of sceptics who had cast doubt on his artistic aspirations, further fueling the seeds of uncertainty that had already settled within him. Lesedi frequently pondered his worthiness of success and whether he possessed the necessary qualities to overcome the challenges that enveloped him.

In Lesedi's mind, a chorus of doubt grew louder and more insistent with each passing day.

Despite the unwavering support of his family, friends, and relatives, he couldn't help but feel like an imposter, questioning whether their belief in his talent and dreams was truly justified.

His mother's undying love and encouragement, his brother's fatherly guidance, and the well-meaning words of friends and relatives, although intended to inspire, occasionally felt overwhelming. Their uncertainties and scepticism, even when disguised with smiles and words of caution, contributed to the burden of self-doubt that plagued him.

***

It was a late night, the room dimly lit by a single lamp as Lesedi immersed himself in his sketches. He pondered whether he truly deserved their unshakeable belief in his talents. Was he truly capable of becoming the artist they envisioned? The echoes of encouragement from his family clashed with the haunting whispers of uncertainty in his mind.

Murmured to himself, "Can I truly fulfill their expectations? Do I possess the necessary qualities to become the artist they envision in me?"

In his meticulous etching, every stroke captured the essence of the township's struggles. However, with each line he drew, a wave of uncertainty crept into his mind.

"You can't," a voice of doubt murmured.

Lesedi's fingers, typically steady, quivered as uncertainty eroded his self-assurance.

"You won't," scoffed self-doubt as he depicted the challenges faced by his community, each stroke of the brush becoming increasingly uncertain.

"You're not good enough," mocked the shadows of his insecurities, as he poured his heart and soul onto the canvas, burdened by the weight of inadequacy that weighed down his artistic spirit.

The room was enveloped in a profound stillness, with only the faint sound of his pencil gliding across the paper and the gentle clinking of paintbrushes. Lesedi found himself caught in a fierce struggle between his lofty ambitions and the relentless chorus of self-doubt, which threatened to dim the vibrant dreams he once held dear.

Lesedi found himself locked in a constant battle between his dreams and the unyielding grip of doubt. This internal struggle seemed to have no end in sight, leaving him feeling uncertain and unsure. The fear of falling short, the nagging worry that he would disappoint those who believed in him, chipped away at his determination, leaving him feeling drained of confidence and hope.

Every day seemed to be a never-ending journey through a dark and discouraging landscape.

When he faced his sketchbook or canvas, a sense of uncertainty weighed him down. The empty pages and canvases taunted him, reminding him that he lacked talent, skill, and worth.

Failure, in all its haunting forms, seemed to always be present.

The fear of disappointing his mother, who had made countless sacrifices for his dreams, was a constant presence in his mind. The weight of the expectations from his friends and relatives, who saw him as a symbol of hope in a place where hope was rare, felt like a heavy burden that could easily drown him in self-doubt.

His internal monologue was filled with pessimism that seemed to never cease.

It constantly reminded him that he was bound to mediocrity, destined to always fall short and that his art would forever be a futile attempt at self-deception.

He seemed to be trapped in a never-ending cycle of negativity, with discouragement and doubt overshadowing any positive thoughts or words of encouragement. It was as if a heavy cloud of self-doubt had taken up residence in his mind, making it difficult to see any flicker of hope or belief in himself.

In the face of mounting doubt, Lesedi's outlook on life became increasingly pessimistic. The vibrant hues that once adorned his sketches now appeared dull, reflecting his diminishing hope. He pondered whether his art had the power to create any meaningful impact in a world where poverty and challenges appeared insurmountable.

Like an artist who had lost his way, he found himself at a crossroads. The weight of sadness and a feeling of being stuck held him back from expressing his creativity. It was as if he was caught in a cycle of monotony, unable to grasp the elusive dreams that danced just out of reach.

Lesedi's artistic passion waned, resembling a sunset losing its brilliance, leaving him with a lingering feeling of emptiness. His sketchbook, once a source of comfort and familiarity, now sat neglected on a shelf, a forgotten artefact of his dreams. Its untouched pages stood in stark contrast to the vibrant township scenes he used to bring to life with unflagging enthusiasm.

He felt trapped, unable to find inspiration or joy in his art. The tools that used to bring him so much happiness now felt burdensome, as if they were holding him back from achieving his dreams. Doubt and uncertainty consumed him, making it difficult to escape from this temporary setback.

Like a dormant flame, his creativity lay hidden, overshadowed by his own doubts.

The absence of art in his life left a void that nothing else could fill. Each passing day without creating was a gradual erosion of the passion he once embraced.

The vibrant colours and vivid tales that once flowed effort-lessly from his sketches now seemed distant, as if mere whispers from a fading past. The creative flame that once burned brightly within him now flickered in the distance; a fading ember that appeared almost impossible to rekindle.

In the eyes of his brother, Thabo, and Kgalalelo, Lesedi's passion seemed to fade away, leaving behind a heavy cloud of self-doubt and the weight of their difficult circumstances. They recognized that art was more than just technical expertise; it was a reflection of the artist's soul, and Lesedi's spirit had become weighed down by his own perceived shortcomings.

During this time, Lesedi's family stood by him, providing steadfast support. They recalled the path he had embarked on, and the optimism and motivation he had brought to their community. They recognized that artistic development often had its ups and downs and that the moments of struggle were just as significant as the moments of triumph.

Thabo, in particular, shared stories of artists he admired, recounting their moments of despair and creative block. He emphasized that even the greatest artists faced periods of self-doubt but had found a way to overcome them. "Art," he said, "is not just about success; it's about the process of creation. It's all about discovering your unique voice and spreading it to the world."

Lesedi's journey through this challenging phase of self-doubt and creative stagnation was intensely affecting his personal life. He recognized that to reignite his passion, he was required to face his fears, self-criticism, and the harsh realities of life in Sebokeng.

Chapter 5: The Enigmatic Painter

In the midst of Lesedi's artistic break, where his sketchbook gathered dust and the colours of his dreams lost their vibrancy, a captivating turn of events took place. On a sombre afternoon, burdened by self-doubt, Lesedi stumbled upon an unknown location - a serene alleyway where the vibrant hues of Sebokeng appeared to lose their lustre.

As he explored this unknown land, there was a distinct and electrifying atmosphere in the air. His doubt enveloped him, a constant reminder that the fantastical had no room in the unforgiving realm of his existence. However, destiny had other intentions in store.

The narrow alley, reminiscent of a hidden corner in the heart of Sebokeng, murmured stories of neglect and abandonment. The sunlight fought to break through the heavy layer of dust that clung stubbornly to the windows of what seemed to be a forgotten art studio. It felt as if the spirit of imagination had abandoned this particular place.

Lesedi, captivated by an indescribable force, found himself drawn to the farthest reaches of the alley. He felt an irresistible pull, a mysterious force compelling him to venture into the long-forgotten corners of an abandoned studio. Uncertainty permeated the air, clinging to Lesedi as he cautiously approached the door that emitted a faint creak.

As he gently nudged the door open, the hinges let out a chorus of creaks, as if they were telling a story of neglect and abandonment. The room that lay before him seemed frozen in time, untouched by the hands of the clock. The atmosphere within exuded a nostalgic aroma, a blend of faded paint, aged canvases, and the faint whispers of creative pursuits from days gone by.

The windows, reminiscent of a forgotten past, cast a soft, gentle light into the room.

It had a mesmerising glow, as if tiny specks of dust were gracefully floating in the air, resembling delicate fireflies. The light brought the forgotten canvases in the studio to life, creating a subtle glow around every brushstroke of colour.

Canvases were propped against easels, caught in different stages of creation as if time had come to a halt. Brushes, once used with great fervour, now find solace in jars, their bristles still bearing the marks of creative expression. A lone chair, adorned with a worn fabric, remained a silent observer of the journey of numerous artists.

As he ventured deeper into this creative haven, an intriguing aura surrounded him.

The atmosphere, reminiscent of a timeless era, hummed

with murmurs of untold tales. The studio, with its worn-out appearance, seemed to beckon to a soul in search of artistic rejuvenation.

The abandoned studio morphed into a conduit, like a storyteller, connecting the forgotten tales of the past with the yearning to be told in the present. Lesedi, immersed in the swirling whirlwind of inspiration, felt a wave of excitement. Unbeknownst to him, this often disregarded area contained the secret to embarking on a fresh phase in his artistic expedition.

In a secluded corner of the room, a gentle radiance appeared as if it had been patiently anticipating an audience. Initially, Lesedi brushed it off, thinking it was just a trick of the lighting. He thought it was a clever deception created by his exhausted mind, an illusion born from the tiredness that clung to him relentlessly.

Still, the radiance remained, unfazed by Lesedi's doubt. It started to change, leaving behind its shy nature for a more captivating appearance. The soft glow of the light turned into a captivating display of colours, transcending the ordinary confines of the room. It felt as though the atmosphere had been infused with a captivating energy, reminiscent of a mystical brilliance.

Unfamiliar hues danced gracefully in the dimness, creating a mesmerising display of shimmering beauty that lingered in the atmosphere with an ethereal touch. Colours of the sky blended harmoniously with the earth, forming mesmerising designs that appeared to follow a divine dance. The play of light created a fleeting masterpiece, a breathtaking display that went beyond the usual and embraced the extraordinary.

Lesedi, captivated by the ethereal spectacle, couldn't look away, his eyes filled with awe. The atmosphere surrounding him was filled with a tangible electricity, and the studio, once enveloped in a state of neglect, now throbbed with an indescribable liveliness.

He could feel the intensity of the glow, knowing deep down that this was no ordinary occurrence. It felt like a manifestation of pure creativity, appearing in a way that was impossible to fully grasp. The room buzzed with an intangible anticipation, hinting at the imminent arrival of something truly remarkable.

At that very moment, caught between the familiar and the unfamiliar, Lesedi experienced a surge of inquisitiveness. The radiant light, akin to a divine mentor, enticed him deeper into the core of the studio, offering insights that surpassed the limits of his creativity. Unbeknownst to him, this radiant occurrence held the answer to unveiling the enchanting realm of his creative fate.

His doubt slowly enveloped him, casting a shadow of scepticism over the enchanting scene before him. He looked intently, his eyes filled with a blend of intrigue and doubt. Intrigued by the persistent glow, undeterred by his initial hesitation, Lesedi cautiously approached the captivating source of this mesmerising radiance.

As he approached, a sense of anticipation filled his chest. In the midst of the radiant light, hovering effortlessly as if challenging the laws of physics, rested a paintbrush. This tool possessed a unique quality that set it apart from others used by artists.

It emitted a radiant glow as if the embodiment of imagination had materialised.

The brush seemed to radiate with a captivating energy that far exceeded what was possible of the physical realm. A gentle hum reverberated throughout the studio as if the entire cosmos recognised the exceptional essence of this very moment.

His eyes widened in surprise.

He hesitated, extending his hand cautiously as if half-expecting the brush in front of him to vanish like the mist at dawn. However, his fingers gently touched the smooth, sturdy handle of the brush. It felt incredibly authentic, and the sensation sent an electrifying chill down his back.

The bristles of the brush, with a touch of magic, appeared to soak up the soft light surrounding them as if they were a painter's canvas capturing the hues of a new day. Every bristle possessed its own distinct colour, effortlessly merging together to create a mesmerising array of shades that reflected the play of light in the room.

In that fleeting moment, Lesedi experienced a profound resonance—a deep connection to something that transcended his comprehension. Inspired by the enchanting world of imagination, the artist's paintbrush emanated a subtle yet captivating energy, inviting him to explore unexplored realms within his creative spirit.

The studio now emanated with the vibrant energy of artistic inspiration.

As he grasped the enchanted paintbrush, a deep sense of realisation washed over him.

His initial scepticism made into an overwhelming feeling of awe and wonder.

He found himself on the cusp of a life-changing adventure, inspired by the radiant power of a paintbrush that could bring his artistic dreams to fruition. His hushed words lingered in the air, a delicate question amidst the extraordinary spectacle unravelling before him.

The Voice, reminiscent of the delicate breeze, replied with

words that held a mystical significance, echoing the vibrant atmosphere of the studio.

"Am I dreaming?" Lesedi pondered, his voice barely audible, a hesitant acknowledgment of doubt.

The Voice, a profound presence that appeared to radiate from the very core of the enchanted paintbrush, replied with a profound wisdom that surpassed the mundane. "In every artist's journey," it whispered, its voice gently caressing the air like a soft breeze, "there is a moment when the mundane moves beyond into something extraordinary. Will you embrace the enchantment that lies within?"

The words hung in the air, caught in the electric atmosphere of the studio.

Lesedi, with the enchanted paintbrush in his hand, sensed a change deep within. It felt as though the universe had presented a question, not only to his mind but to the depths of his soul. The physical reality seemed to fade away, leaving behind only the vibrant aura of the enchanting brush and the serene echo of a captivating voice.

In the quiet studio, illuminated by a gentle, ethereal glow, Lesedi found himself at a crossroads. Inspired by the enchantment of the unknown, the artist's brush became a gateway to a realm where art defied its conventional limitations, leaving doubt and scepticism behind.

His heart filled with a mixture of doubt and excitement, silently made a promise.

Inspired by the mystical encounter, the mysterious Voice, and the vibrant brushstrokes, Lesedi's artistry embarked on an unforgettable journey, delving into the depths of the ordinary world to reveal its extraordinary essence.

The enchanting paintbrush floated in front of Lesedi, as if it existed in a realm between the physical and the spiritual. The bristles had a captivating quality, emitting a gentle radiance that hinted at the power of change.

Lesedi, standing on the edge of doubt and intrigue, felt the heaviness of the mundane world enveloping him. In this singular moment, the convergence of the dusty art studio, the narrow alley, and the struggles of the township creates a blurred boundary between reality and enchantment.

A soft murmur filled the studio, as if a gentle breeze carried a tale of endless potential. "Yet," it whispered, the word filled with an enigmatic conviction, "the enchanted paintbrush they presented carried a pledge." The atmosphere crackled with possibility, and Lesedi couldn't help but feel a tingle of excitement creep up his back.

Drawn into the promise held by the enchanted bristles of the paintbrush, Lesedi felt captivated by its otherworldly radiance. It ignored being just a tool, opening up a gateway to a realm where the limitations of Sebokeng faded away in the face of something extraordinary.

The Voice suggested a voyage, a grand adventure that would take Lesedi far from the familiar streets and challenging realities of his hometown. It evoked a sense of destiny intertwined with bursts of imagination, of a limitless canvas that extended far beyond the pages of his sketchbook. The promise went far beyond individual achievements; it delved into the essence of existence itself.

In that moment, Lesedi was filled with an unflagging resolve. Just as an artist's doubts can sometimes fade away, his artistic vision was momentarily illuminated by the enchanting power of the paintbrush. Inspired by the magic of his craft, Lesedi found himself standing at the precipice of a remarkable crossroads.

With his aspirations weighing heavily on his shoulders, he knew that this ordinary alleyway had the potential to become a gateway to something extraordinary.

In the dimly lit alley, Lesedi's footsteps reverberated as he emerged from the abandoned art studio, clutching the enchanted paintbrush in his hands. The gentle glow emanating from it seemed to extend far beyond its bristles, delicately illuminating the worn path beneath his feet.

As he strolled, the township revealed itself like a vivid portrait of hardship and determination. The faces of neighbours and friends welcomed him, their expressions a blend of curiosity and familiarity. There was a certain aura surrounding Lesedi, a subtle change in the atmosphere that hinted at a profound connection to the world of creativity.

In the distance stood his own home, a place where the burdens of poverty and the haunting echoes of his stepfather's words had attempted to smother his aspirations. Clutching the enchanted paintbrush in his hand, it radiated with the potential for incredible change.

Upon stepping foot into his humble abode, the ambiance underwent a noticeable transformation. In the dimly lit room, a space that had witnessed its fair share of challenges, there existed the promise of something truly remarkable. His mother, brother, and even his mentally ill uncle paused in their daily routines, sensing a captivating energy that surpassed the ordinary.

Lesedi, with the enchanted paintbrush in his hand, locked eyes with his family.

His mother's eyes gleamed with optimism, his brother silently urged him on, and even his uncle's wandering gaze momentarily found its purpose.

The Voice, reminiscent of a gentle whisper that lingers in the air, spoke directly to Lesedi's heart. "Embrace the enchantment that resides within," it echoed. His work had moved past its humble origins and now embodied something truly remarkable.

Immersed in the enchanting power of the paintbrush, Lesedi experienced a profound sense of doubt dissipating. In the depths of his humble abode, once a breeding ground for challenges, an incredible shift took place. As he took each step, he wasn't merely heading home; he was entering the crossroads of his fate, where his inner magic would infuse the mundane with life and add strokes of hope to the tapestry of his existence.

With a sense of anticipation, Lesedi cautiously removed the cap from the enchanted paintbrush. It radiated a gentle, otherworldly light, casting a luminous glow on the artwork that adorned his walls. His heart beat with a mixture of excitement and trepidation as he delicately touched the brush to a palette filled with an array of vivid hues.

The initial stroke displayed a sense of caution as if the brush was exploring the depths of Lesedi's artistic potential. Incredibly, the paint glided effortlessly onto the canvas, radiating a brilliance that exceeded all previous encounters.

As he continued, the paintbrush seemed to effortlessly aid his hand, transforming simple lines and colours into a captivating display of emotions. However, obstacles presented themselves. Lesedi found himself captivated by the brush, which seemed to possess a magical quality that demanded an unprecedented level of focus and connection. It captured the subtle shifts in his emotions, transforming the murmurs of his innermost being into vibrant brushstrokes on the canvas.

There were moments when the brush seemed to possess a life of its own, crafting intricate patterns and textures that went beyond the boundaries of conventional artistry. The magical paintbrush demanded that Lesedi embrace a sense of vulnerability and allow himself to be guided by unseen forces in order to unleash its extraordinary creative power.

He would often find himself engaged in a captivating battle of determination whenever the brush didn't cooperate with his vision. He would pause, inhale deeply, and the brush's radiance would pulsate in answer. It felt like creativity itself was seeking a perfect partnership between the artist and their magical instrument.

The obstacles, although intimidating, served as catalysts for Lesedi's artistic development. He honed his skills in understanding the intricate dance of this ethereal bond. Inspired by the enchanting power of a paintbrush, Lesedi's artwork became a captivating expression of his deepest emotions and musings.

As he painted, the room became infused with a mystical aura. The sketches on the walls seemed to come alive, their stories unfolding with a newfound depth and richness.

The everyday moments of Sebokeng's life took on a vibrant quality, becoming stories filled with hope, resilience, and the profoundness of art.

His adventure with the enchanted paintbrush was a beautiful exploration, a series of obstacles and victories that resonated with the inner magic he possessed. The canvas came alive under his skilled hand, revealing a world of endless possibilities and untold stories.

His creativity soared as the magical paintbrush became an ethereal extension, guiding him into uncharted realms of imagination. As he painted, the room took on a mystical quality, as if it existed beyond the bounds of reality. The walls turned into a surreal realm, where every brushstroke created gateways to unexplored dimensions.

He effortlessly brought forth vivid scenes that defied the boundaries of reality.

In these enchanting landscapes, colours danced in perfect harmony, mythical creatures came alive with every breath, and captivating narratives unfolded like chapters in a celestial storybook. The mesmerising brushstrokes possessed a unique language, crafting stories that resonated with the secrets of existence.

The atmosphere was filled with the enchantment that Lesedi effortlessly created. His sketches, much like the work of a visionary artist, broke free from the confines of paper and ventured into realms beyond the ordinary.

It felt as though a mystical paintbrush had unlocked a portal to a world where the lines between artist and creation melded together, and the act of painting turned into a cosmic dance.

In the solitude of his room, Lesedi experienced a sense of relief as his doubts and self-criticism slowly faded away, much like the mist that disappeared with the rising sun. The enchanted paintbrush, like a wise mentor, accompanied him on a profound voyage of self-exploration, leading him through the boundless realms of his untapped abilities. Every brushstroke was a journey into uncharted territory, a quest to uncover the boundless potential at his fingertips.

However, the enigmatic experience presented its own set of difficulties. Lesedi felt the weight of the immense power he possessed. He struggled to come to terms with the fact that every action had repercussions, molding not just his own world but the fabric of existence itself. The enchantment possessed a duality, requiring reverence and focus in its utilisation.

In the soft illumination of the moonlight, seeping through his window, Lesedi found himself captivated by the extraordinary creation that lay before him. He couldn't help but be in awe of the profound transformation he had experienced. Inspired by the mystical wonders of the universe, the room radiated with a mesmerising palette that surpassed the boundaries of perception. It was here that his artistic journey unfolded, blending the mundane with the extraordinary.

In Lesedi's hands, the paintbrush seemed to possess a vibrant energy, as if it held the essence of creation itself. The artist found himself on the cusp of a world where imagination came to life through art. From humble beginnings, the boy from the township of Sebokeng was ready to embrace his remarkable future as a master of his craft.

Similar to an artist who undergoes an incredible journey, Lesedi's perception of art was forever changed when he held the enchanted paintbrush. He felt the revolutionary nature of each brushstroke, expanding his perception of the creative journey. Inspired by the enigmatic wonders of the universe, his art transcended the boundaries of the physical world, changing into a captivating expression of the ethereal.

He was led by an enchanting brush that took him on a journey through realms where colours were imbued with emotions, and shapes whispered captivating stories.

Lesedi realised that art went beyond mere expression; it was a profound conversation with the invisible energies that ignited his creativity. The ethereal encounters within his sketches transcended the boundaries of imagination and resonated with the essence of life itself.

In his perception, his creations moved beyond being mere drawings. They became portals to emotions, connections to hidden realms, and reflections of the vast spectrum of human experiences. In the realm of artistic expression, the paintbrush possessed an enchanting power to reveal the profound connection between the creator and their creation. Every stroke carried the artist's deepest emotions, which in turn, stirred a profound resonance within those who looked at the artwork.

The idea of perfection vanished amidst the enchanting colours. Imperfections changed into charming quirks that brought depth to the story. The canvas became a realm where creativity and spontaneity intertwined, and missteps became unexpected moments of fortune. Lesedi fully embraced the concept that art is a continuous journey, where each piece captures a moment in the ever-changing expedition.

His approach to the creative process underwent a metamorphosis, moving away from meticulous planning and embracing the realm of spontaneous exploration. Inspired by the enchanting power of art, he trusted his intuition and allowed the creative energies to effortlessly flow through him. The studio exuded an air of mystery and possibility, where the conventional of art was surpassed by the allure of the extraordinary.

Inspiration flowed through his veins, silencing the doubts that had haunted his artistic pursuits. The paintbrush became a conduit for his creativity, altering his doubts into a symphony of artistic expression. Lesedi's art took on a mystical quality, a fusion of talent, passion, and the ethereal energy that coursed through his being. The canvas turned from a mere surface for images into a gateway to the artist's innermost being.

With his newfound perspective, Lesedi became a source of inspiration for the local artist community. His work captivated even the most sceptical peers, who were in awe of its ethereal quality. Inspired by the enchanting power of the paintbrush, Lesedi's art underwent a remarkable transformation, igniting a wave of creativity that swept through the entire Sebokeng.

In Lesedi's life, a chapter unfolded that surpassed the limits of reality, like a masterpiece on a tapestry. Inspired by the enchanting allure of the universe, his artistic journey unfolded with a touch of magic, turning the mundane into something truly extraordinary. From humble beginnings, he blossomed into a masterful conductor, orchestrating his own celestial symphony.

Lesedi's possession of the enchanted paintbrush turned his ordinary days into a canvas of boundless possibilities. As he entered the well-known street of the township, the enchanting brush reshaped into a versatile instrument of creativity. It effortlessly transformed into the perfect tool for his creative vision, whether it be a pencil, a charcoal stick, or any other artistic instrument he imagined.

As he strolled through the vibrant streets, the ordinary sights around him became a canvas for his imaginative musings. In his mind's eye, he imagined a meticulous pencil sketch, and as if by magic, the paintbrush morphed into a pencil, skillfully capturing every minute detail with the expertise of a seasoned draughtsman. The brush effortlessly changed into a vibrant palette, just as an artist inspired by the world around them, infusing life into every corner of the township.

The process flowed effortlessly, a harmonious interplay of ideas and manifestation. Lesedi discovered that he no longer required a vast collection of art materials. Instead, he found that his imagination could effortlessly shape the brush to match the ever-shifting landscapes of his mind. If a mural graced the side of a building in his imagination, the brush would effortlessly glide across the canvas, transforming the urban landscape into a vivid loom of hues.

Passersby was captivated by Lesedi's seamless transition between different artistic mediums, witnessing the enchanting brush effortlessly bringing his creative vision to life. The walls of the township turned into a vibrant gallery, showcasing the limitless possibilities that emerged with every stroke of the magical tool.

However, it wasn't solely about the brush's physical changes; it encompassed the graceful flow of artistic expression. An artist with a versatile brush, he effortlessly adapted his strokes to capture the essence of his creative vision.

The artistic community now stood in awe of the profound connection between Lesedi and his enchanted tool. Inspired by the spirit of Sebokeng, his sketches captured the essence of a world beyond the physical, each stroke giving life to a story that resonated deeply.

In the secluded depths of his studio, Lesedi delved into the boundless potential that the enchanted brush bestowed upon him. With a boundless imagination, he effortlessly transformed his tools to match his creative vision. The brush morphed into a chisel, allowing him to sculpt with precision and passion. And when he yearned to capture the fleeting moments of life, his camera became a powerful instrument, freezing the essence of motion in timeless photographs.

His creativity transcended the boundaries of traditional art, expanding into the realm of the extraordinary. Inspired by the enchanting power of a paintbrush, the township turned into a vast canvas, brimming with endless possibilities for artistic expression.

Within his element, Lesedi skillfully navigated the well-known streets, wielding his enchanted brush. Inspiration flowed effortlessly from his every step as if his brush held the power to weave a mesmerising work of creativity.

Inspired by the magic of imagination, the ordinary houses

underwent a breathtaking metamorphosis, becoming magnificent masterpieces adorned with captivating murals that beautifully narrated the rich history, vibrant present, and hopeful aspirations of the township. The streets came alive with a vibrant energy as if creativity itself filled the air.

As Lesedi immersed himself in his artistic pursuits, Sebokeng experienced a profound change. The lines between the realms of imagination and reality became indistinguishable, resulting in a captivating blend of the magical and the concrete. People passing by found themselves unknowingly becoming part of this artistic masterpiece, as their ordinary lives intertwined with the ever-growing tapestry of Lesedi's creation.

The worn-out wall became a portal to a different dimension, adorned with mesmerising patterns that murmured stories of the cosmos. Walking through the streets felt like stepping into a vibrant gallery, where every corner revealed a new masterpiece painted by an enchanting brush.

The townsfolk, amazed by Lesedi's artistic talent, were captivated by the vibrant display of creativity that unfolded in front of them. Just like a master storyteller, the brush made ordinary fences into magnificent golden gates, and hidden alleyways into portals to extraordinary realms. Sebokeng itself transformed into a vibrant work of art, moulded by the magical touch of Lesedi's artistic talent.

In the enchanting moonlight, Lesedi's paintbrush danced with life, making the night's canvas into a celestial spectacle. Stars twinkle like precious gems, illuminating the brick walls and creating a gentle, otherworldly radiance that envelops the streets. Lesedi's feet tread upon the asphalt, which now sparkled with constellations that once only graced the night sky. As he journeyed through the township, the vibrant dreams that emanated from his imaginative mind materialised in brilliant colours.

The night became a vibrant canvas of ethereal allure.

Every brushstroke seemed to possess a touch of magic, leaving behind a trail of stardust that turned the canvas into a mesmerising celestial display, enchanting all who beheld it.

The constellations seemed to come alive, weaving tales that went beyond the ordinary.

A radiant phoenix glided gracefully across a canvas of bricks, its wings spread wide as it soared through eternity. The pathways came alive with the enchanting presence of mythical creatures, their ethereal forms painted in shades of moonlit blues and silver. They gracefully danced, spinning tales of magic and wonder that captivated all who beheld them.

The ethereal dreams stretched far beyond the confines of the city, enveloping the majestic trees in their radiant embrace. The leaves glowed with a celestial brilliance, as though they were infused with the magic of the cosmos. The night air itself seemed to vibrate with the melodies of the universe, a beautiful dance of illumination and darkness guided by Lesedi's artistic brilliance.

The townsfolk were captivated by a mesmerising world that went beyond their ordinary existence. The night had turned into a captivating masterpiece, a harmonious blend of the artist's touch and the allure of a mystical brush. As Lesedi wandered through the streets, his figure seamlessly blended into the vibrant illumination surrounding him.

He glided with the grace of a maestro, effortlessly choreographing a mesmerising dance of illumination that unfolded with every stride. Inspired by the captivating allure he had unleashed, it became more than just a spectacle. It became an open invitation for the community to embark on a journey of dreams, to embrace the enchanting magic that lies within even the darkest corners of their existence.

In the stillness of the night, the ethereal dreams created by Lesedi's enchanted paintbrush murmured of uncharted horizons, of a destiny moulded by the boundless power of artistic creativity. Inspired by the magic of imagination, the streets came alive with a captivating aura, illuminating the night with the radiance of countless constellations.

With a touch of enchantment, Lesedi's brush brought forth a mesmerising dance that not only transformed his surroundings but also stirred the hearts of those fortunate enough to witness the magic. Sebokeng radiated with the brilliance of optimism and the potential for artistic expression.

Lesedi's artistic journey was more than just a personal endeavour; it united the township in wonder and motivation. The streets, once stagnant, now bear witness to the boundless potential of imagination, demonstrating that even in the face of adversity, the human soul can transcend the boundaries of the ordinary, propelled by the enchantment of artistic manifestation.

In the midst of the enchanting masterpieces created by an extraordinary artist, Lesedi discovered himself traversing the otherworldly realms of his own imagination. The streets, reminiscent of the works of a renowned author, seemed to come alive with a captivating and ethereal aura, as if the spirit of imagination had permeated every inch of the pavement.

In perfect synchrony, the brush glided with effortless elegance, giving life to a world that surpassed the confines of our imagination. The trees seemed to whisper with the mysteries of the universe, their leaves capturing the ethereal beauty of Lesedi's mesmerising brushstrokes. Flowers burst forth in a mesmerising array of colours and shapes, their petals whispering tales of the hopes and aspirations that were intricately entwined within their fragile beauty.

Lesedi's art touched the souls of those fortunate enough to witness his captivating nighttime display. The townsfolk were enthralled by the captivating visual feast that lay before them. However, as time went on, they discovered a profound connection to the luminescent dreams that went beyond mere aesthetics. The mesmerising scenes became reflections of their own hopes, anxieties, and undiscovered capabilities.

A gathering emerged amidst the altered streets—residents, acquaintances, and unfamiliar faces brought together by the enchanting allure of Lesedi's extraordinary creations. Laughter mixed with wonder as children pursued ethereal butterflies that appeared and disappeared. The elders gazed at the constellations adorning the walls, reliving the timeless tales that had been handed down for generations.

However, in the midst of the enchantment, a deep silence hung in the air, as if everyone present understood that something truly remarkable was taking place. Lesedi had become the vessel through which the community's shared aspirations were given voice. His art went beyond being a mere spectacle. It became a collective tribute to the indomitable spirit of the township, showcasing its ability to rise above challenges through the power of imagination. In the midst of the unfolding dreams, Lesedi experienced a deep sense of connection to his community. In the realm of artistic creation, the brush spanned its mere function and became a conduit that connected souls and thoughts. He had a unique ability to connect with people on a deep level, touched their hearts and minds with his artistic expression.

The enigmatic Figure, who had gifted Lesedi with the enchanted paintbrush, watched silently from the darkness. Their true nature remained hidden, yet an air of deep insight and kindness enveloped them. They had not only given Lesedi a brush, but had sparked a fire that would ignite the entire Sebokeng with the power of beautiful art.

* * *

Lesedi finds himself in his humble art studio, with a trusty paint-brush by his side. Thabo and Kgalalelo watch with fascination as they observe the unflagging dedication with which Lesedi works.

Thabo gently tapped Kgalalelo, "Look at your last born son in action. It looks like he's making dreams come true on that painting."

Kgalalelo smiled, "Thabo, his zeal is back. He seems to be coming to life in everything he's doing."

As Lesedi was painting, the room bursts with the vivid colours of his imagination. The waves shimmer and collide against unseen shores, while graceful birds soar through the boundless expanse of the atmosphere.

Thabo spoke in a low voice, "I think he's onto something big."

Kgalalelo agreed, "Inspired by the challenges he has faced, his spirit remains unbroken, fueling his boundless creativity."

Lesedi's self-doubt is silenced as his brush dances across the canvas, creating a world of enchantment.

Lesedi's mother cheered "Keep going, you're doing great!"

"You're creating a world that remains hidden from our sight. But I can feel it. It's as if you've discovered a path to rise above the all odds."

Lesedi gazes upwards, his eyes shining with the enchantment of his craft.

"I am filled with gratitude." Lesedi whisper to himself

It's as if the brush is intimately acquainted with the tales these walls yearn to share. I am merely the narrator.

Like a guiding light, a mother's love shines bright. Emotionally moved, the mother spoke, "My kid, you are building a universe where our aspirations have room to flourish."

As Lesedi continues to paint, Thabo and Kgalalelo exchange approving looks. They have a deep understanding of the meaning behind the painted strokes; they bear witness to the emergence of hope, strength, and an inexorable commitment to transform challenges into works of art.

* * *

Lesedi walks confidently through the familiar streets, his paintbrush held with purpose. For others, it may be seen as a mundane tool, but for Lesedi, it unlocks a realm of enchantment.

Thabo with a smile, "Are you still taking that brush with you everywhere, brother?"

As Lesedi walks, he begins to create a masterpiece on an unseen canvas in the air. The brick walls are adorned with vibrant flowers that emit a soft glow, while the pavement below is illuminated by a mesmerising river of stars.

Like a guiding force, a mother's love and care are unparalleled. She is there to nurture, protect, and support her children, always putting their needs above her own. A mother's presence is a source of comfort and strength, providing guidance and wisdom along

Thabo curiously asked, "What is the colour? Where is it?"

Lesedi chuckles, relishing the hidden realm that is uniquely his.

"Here, Thabo. Do you not perceive the stars? What about the flowers? "

Thabo narrows his eyes, gazing at the seemingly vacant area. Perplexed, "Stars? Flowers? Do you ever take a moment to consider if you might be pushing yourself too much? "

Lesedi smiles, opting to savour the enchantment privately. Lesedi happily, responded, "Perhaps I perceive things that elude others. Believe me, it's truly exquisite."

As they continue their walk, Lesedi's brush effortlessly creates ethereal scenes. The town becomes a tapestry of aspirations, hidden from those who stroll alongside the painter with the unassuming brush.

* * *

Inspired by the enchanting power of art, Lesedi's brush brings forth a radiant glow that fills the studio with a captivating and lively atmosphere. The walls are decorated with paintings that capture the vibrant dreams he has brought to life on the streets. Lesedi is lost in his own world, completely absorbed in his artistic process.

Lesedi's mother enters, captivated by the enchanting scenes immortalised on canvas.

Kgalalelo was captivated by her last born's work, "Lesedi, my son, these paintings... They take me to another dimension, opening up a completely novel worldview. How are you able to accomplish it?"

With a tranquil expression, he delicately dips the brush into a vibrant palette of colours.

"There is a certain magic in the everyday, Mama. The streets whisper to me, and this brush... It turns their whispers into beams of brightness."

Like a guiding force, a mother's love and care are unparalleled. She is there to nurture, protect, and support us through life's ups and downs. Her presence is a constant source of strength and inspiration, reminding us to always strive for the best version with tears in her eyes, "You're truly remarkable, my son."

Lesedi lets out a small laugh, his voice carrying a touch of humility, "We're working together, Mama. I create art that is deeply rooted in my emotions, and the community graciously shares their stories, which I then bring to life on the canvas. The enchantment lies not only within the strokes of the brush but also within the captivating tales of our township. Observe carefully, and you will witness the aspirations of those around us, the strength of our collective spirit."

Like an artist capturing the essence of the world, the scene on the canvas perfectly reflects the streets beyond. The walls are adorned with flowers that emit a soft glow, while the pavement is adorned with twinkling stars.

Thabo steps into the room, his eyes widening in awe as he takes in the incredible transformation of the studio.

Thabo was astonished by Lesedi works, "Lesedi, this is truly amazing. You've transformed the entire town into a work of art."

Lesedi gazing upwards, "Thabo, the enchantment extends beyond my own self. It's a universal experience. I desire for the streets to become a blank canvas where everyone's dreams can come to life."

Thabo acknowledged, fully grasping the profound influence his brother's art has on the community.

"You're creating something beyond mere paintings, Lesedi. You inspire a sense of hope." Lesedi smiles, the brush glowing with anticipation for another stroke.

Through every brushstroke, he stated, "We create a vision of the future that goes beyond our hardships."

Lesedi on the street in Sebokeng during the day.

Lesedi perches on a weathered stool, clutching his sketchbook, capturing the very soul of Sebokeng. In his hand, the paintbrush possesses an enchanting quality, unseen by those who observe.

An inquisitive neighbour approached Lesedi, "What drives you to dedicate your days to painting every day without fail? Why not explore alternative paths?"

Lesedi smiled, "These streets hold a deeper meaning. They are like blank canvases, ready to weave tales."

The neighbour, perplexed, gazed at the unremarkable paintbrush in Lesedi's hand. "I know you have a passion for art, but have you considered the potential financial opportunities in other fields? "

Thoughtfully Lesedi answered, "There is more to life than just financial wealth. Every brushstroke holds a profound meaning. This work of art serves as a connection between the challenges of life and the aspirations we hold dear. It is a testament to the fact that even in the face of adversity, there is still room for beauty to flourish."

"Is there beauty to be found in hardship? I fail to see it." Neighbour asked curiously.

Lesedi gazes at the bustling township, his eyes filled with a deep sense of tandem with all that is around him.

Lesedi softly spoke, "That's because you're looking solely through your visual senses. I'm creating art that is deeper than what the eyes can see and the mind can comprehend."

As he continues sketching, a profound sense of reflection envelops him. Lesedi starts to ponder the purpose behind his artistic pursuits. Why choose this brush? Why these streets? What is the meaning behind capturing radiant dreams in the midst of darkness?

In Lesedi's room - night

Lesedi is engrossed in his sketchbook, holding a paintbrush that is filled with a touch of magic. Its gentle glow fills the room with a dreamlike ambiance. He admires the sketches of the streets of Sebokeng, every stroke filled with the brilliance of his newfound artistic ability.

His mind is a complex maze of thoughts, with the question resonating like a gentle tune in the peacefulness of his room. He ponders the meaning of his art, the ethereal bond between the brush and his artistic voyage.

Lesedi whispered, "What led you to seek my presence? What is the reason behind illuminating these scenes?" Examining the brush.

The enchanting paintbrush stays quiet, its radiance mirroring the cadence of Lesedi's heart.

In this introspective dialogue, Lesedi explores the essence of his artistic journey.

The following day, his sketches take a captivating twist. He explores the realm of imagination, infusing ordinary moments with a hint of enchantment. Unbeknownst to him, the streets were turned into gateways to ethereal dimensions. Under the enchantment of his brush, the mundane changed into something truly extraordinary. Nevertheless, the portals would shut down as quickly as they appeared.

Amidst the chaos of the bustling marketplace, Lesedi discovered his canvas, a sanctuary for his artistic expression. People rushed through the narrow alleyways, the lively atmosphere of the marketplace filling every nook and cranny. The rich aromas of spices and the lively voices of vendors painted a vivid picture, immersing themselves in the essence of Sebokeng.

His easel, reminiscent of the works of renowned art masters before him, exuded an air of creative enlightenment as it stood proudly amidst the carefully arranged artistic chaos. Inspired by the enchanting world that unfolded before his eyes, the artist's brush was poised and ready, holding the promise of a captivated growth. With a discerning gaze, driven by a deep artistic intuition, he has seen more than what met the eye. Just as a masterful artist sees beyond the ordinary, he perceived the marketplace as a stage ready to host the enchanting spectacle of radiant aspirations.

Inspired by the world around him, he reshaped the once-broken walls into an expansive canvas, telling the stories of time and the struggles of Sebokeng. Every tiny detail became a brushstroke in the story he was about to reveal. The paint flowed effortlessly from the brush to the canvas, creating a mesmerising display of vibrant colours and profound symbolism.

As he painted, the atmosphere around him seemed to come alive with a vibrant energy. Passersby, captivated by the unfolding masterpiece, found themselves unable to resist its allure. The marketplace, reminiscent of the profound beauty found in the works of great authors, now stood still to observe the great power of art. With vendors showcasing their goods, children darting between stalls, and elders finding respite on makeshift benches, it was as if the entire scene had come alive in an unexpected spectacle. The ethereal dreams manifested, weaving tales of strength and optimism that surpassed the mundane.

His brushstrokes beautifully captured the vibrant energy of the marketplace, where the struggles of everyday life were intertwined with moments of resilience. Inspired by the brilliance of the community, the vibrant array of colours reflects the collective strength that arises from overcoming challenges together.

The marketplace, typically driven by the need to survive, now throbbed with a distinct vitality. The ethereal dreams crafted by Lesedi sparked discussions among those who experienced them. The crowd was filled with curiosity, and a sense of wonder spread through the air.

Thabo by the beauty before him, his eyes widen in awe as he witnesses the ethereal dreams coming to life on the canvas. The ordinary streets, now illuminated by Lesedi's art, have transformed into platforms for remarkable stories.

Sebokeng, familiar with tales of hardship, now echoed with murmurs of a new story. Lesedi's artwork brings forgotten corners to life, infusing them with hope and beauty. The streets that were once quiet now throb with the energy of vivid dreams, a powerful reminder of the magic that creativity can bring.

Just like a blossoming flower, Lesedi's art spreads its radiance throughout the township, unveiling its purpose. Inspired by the magic of creation, each stroke of the brush captures the indomitable spirit of humanity and the boundless potential of artistic self-expression.

Guided by the mystical paintbrush, continued to delve into this captivating realm of imagination. Every brushstroke is now a purposeful decision, a stride towards uncovering the enigmas of his craft. The radiant dreams he captured are not mere products of imagination, but pieces of a larger purpose coming into form.

In the serenity of his room, enveloped by vibrant sketches that exude enchantment, Lesedi discovered solace in the elusive revelations whispered by the mystical paintbrush. Immersed in the soft glow of moonlight, Lesedi finds himself captivated by the ethereal visions flowing from his sketches. As he delves into his artistic journey, a mystical paintbrush hovers in the air, silently accompanying him.

Lesedi, in a state of deep contemplation, allows the brush to lead his hand. Every brushstroke brings ordinary scenes to life, turning them into portals to captivating realms. The streets come alive, pulsating with an ethereal energy, beckoning us to catch a glimpse of unimaginable realms.

However, with the fleeting enchantment of every brushstroke, the doorways shut just as quickly as they reveal themselves. Lesedi, entranced by the realms of reality and imagination, gazes intently at the closing gateways, only to witness the miraculous appearance of a Figure on the other side. It exudes an aura of enchanting allure and enigmatic charm, akin to a sentinel of the creative realms.

Lesedi scared murmured, "What... Who are you?"

He is drawn to the mysterious allure of this Figure, an embodiment of boundless imagination that compels him to venture into unexplored realms of his craft. Lesedi, filled with wonder, comes to the realisation that the enchanted paintbrush is more than just a mere instrument - it holds the power to open doors to realms that surpass his wildest dreams.

In the solitude of his room, enveloped by the traces of sealed gateways and radiant aspirations, Lesedi perceives a profound revelation. In the realm of his art, the essence has transformed into an expedition of self-exploration, where every brushstroke serves as a stride towards unravelling the enigmas of creativity.

Just like a masterful artist, Lesedi is on the brink of embarking on a life-changing journey, pushing the boundaries of his creativity. Enticing Lesedi to want to explore the limitless possibilities of their art. Little does he know, the streets of Sebokeng conceal hidden mysteries, eagerly awaiting his arrival into this enchanting realm.

Chapter 6: The Brush's Secret

As Lesedi entered the mystical realm, the ordinary streets of the township morphed into a captivating dreamscape of otherworldly allure. In the realm beyond the veil, the landscapes unfolded with a sense of enchantment and wonder, as if they were pages from a celestial storybook. Trees reached towards the sky, their branches entangled with ethereal particles that twirled and frolicked in the atmosphere. Flowers of extraordinary colours blossomed, their delicate petals emitting a gentle light that adorned the earth with luminous designs.

The sky above resembled a captivating painting, constantly shifting and transforming from the deep blues of twilight to the lively shades of an everlasting sunrise. Celestial bodies, unknown constellations, shimmered and gleamed in perfect synchrony, casting a soft glow upon the captivating scenery beneath.

The meandering rivers of liquid crystal flowed through the surreal landscape, mirroring not only the physical surroundings but also the hopes and dreams of those who journeyed through this otherworldly realm. Imagine bridges woven from ethereal strands, linking enchanting islands that serve as havens for the exploration and exaltation of artistic expression.

As Lesedi entered this enchanting realm, he felt the gentle touch of the earth beneath his feet, a surface that seemed to envelop him in a comforting embrace, as if it held the secrets of countless whispered musings. The atmosphere was filled with the fragrance of potential, and each inhalation held the spirit of undiscovered escapades yearning to be written into being.

Magical beings and fantastical creatures wandered without restraint, effortlessly transitioning between the ordinary and the extraordinary. They possessed a deep understanding of the power of art to elevate the ordinary into something extraordinary, like a modern-day alchemist.

In this realm of enchanting wonder, the boundaries of the tangible world were mere whispers, and the boundless depths of creativity were forever expanding. It was a place where creativity flowed effortlessly, and the connection between the artist and the art merged seamlessly into a captivating masterpiece. Lesedi stood at the threshold of a captivating realm, armed with the brush, eager to embark on a journey through the boundless landscapes of his own imagination.

As Lesedi gazed upon the mysterious Figures in this ethereal dreamscape, the atmosphere seemed to radiate with the colours of undiscovered dreams. The splendent brilliance that radiated from one of the Figures was more than just a trick of the light; it was a tangible representation of imaginative power, a halo that resonated with the limitless potential of artistic creativity.

The landscapes surrounding the Figure appeared to be inspired by the ethereal realms of the mind. The majestic mountains rose proudly, their summits reaching toward the vibrant sky, a masterpiece of boundless emotions. Valleys stretched out before him, their vastness inviting stories of bravery and strength to be woven into their very fabric.

In the realm of imagination, a river flowed gracefully, capturing the essence of unspoken desires and the echoes of creative expression. The trees, with their leaves whispering stories of forgotten thoughts, created shadows that gracefully swayed with the Figure's every step.

The radiant aura of the Figure was dynamic, resembling a flowing stream of inspiration that breathed life into the very fabric of the dream world. They seemed to channel the very essence that ignites the creative soul, transforming abstract concepts into masterful brushstrokes and fleeting notions into vivid hues on the tapestry of existence.

The being effortlessly directed the metamorphosis of the surroundings. The earth beneath their every step, each stride narrated a beautiful tale. Inspired by the enchantment of the world, the air was filled with the sweet scent of unexplored possibilities, as if the very essence of creativity had blossomed. The skies above, a constantly shifting masterpiece, depicted scenes that unfolded like chapters in the story of existence.

As the Figure reached out to Lesedi, the dreamscape itself seemed to react. The enchanting landscapes seemed to come alive with a captivating display of vivid hues, evoking a sense of wonder and awe. The touch of the Figure stirred a profound sense of creative energy that reverberated throughout the entire realm.

The radiant glow emanating from the Figure was more than just light; it embodied the very essence of inspiration. The fantastical landscapes were brought to life, showcasing their inherent beauty and the immense power that could be unlocked with a stroke of a paintbrush. In the realm of artistic expression, the maestro extended an invitation to Lesedi, unveiling the boundless possibilities of his craft.

The heavens above shifted into a celestial masterpiece, with galaxies dancing in mesmerising formations, every star a symbol of the aspirations interwoven into the very essence of existence. The Figure beckoned Lesedi to grasp the profound message behind this celestial spectacle, reminding him that his art possessed the ability to banish the shadows and create uncharted realms.

In this ethereal realm, time seemed to slip, and the lines between the past, present, and future became uncertain. The entity, resembling the essence that lies between the tangible and the ethereal, communicated through a form of expression that surpassed the limitations of mere words. It spoke in a symphony of hues, forms, and sentiments. It was a conversation that resonated deep within Lesedi's being, a profound sense that he stood at the precipice of an extraordinary experience.

As the Figure looked into the distance, the dreamscape underwent another transformation. This time, it portrayed scenes from Lesedi's personal journey—the challenges, the victories, the instances of uncertainty, and the bursts of motivation. Every scene seemed like a chapter ready to be penned, and the mysterious Figure, wearing a wise smile, hinted that Lesedi was the one holding the pen.

Inspired by the artistic gestures, the enchanting realm became a testament to the boundless possibilities that awaited Lesedi.

It was an invitation to embark on a journey of exploration, creativity, and, most importantly, to have faith in the incredible transformative potential of one's own imagination.

The landscapes around them blended the familiar scenes of Lesedi's township with fantastical elements that stretched beyond the limits of imagination. The trees resonated with the melodies of hushed confidences, while the streets throbbed with the rhythm of a world infused with enchantment.

And in this mesmerising moment, between the ordinary and the extraordinary, Lesedi discovered himself on the verge of an artistic journey that surpassed the boundaries of his most extravagant aspirations. Inspired by the spirit of creativity, the streets transformed from a reflection of everyday challenges to a canvas brimming with limitless artistic potential, ready to be brought to life by the stroke of a brush.

The atmosphere was charged with a palpable energy that resonated deeply within the essence of existence. Like a master storyteller, the Figure's features slowly revealed themselves as the ethereal glow faded away. Their face exuded a pearl of profound wisdom, as if they had traversed countless realms and gathered stories from ages past.

Those eyes, filled with boundless imagination, contained entire universes within their stare. They appeared to mirror the tales of artists who had traversed the vast realms of imagination. In just one look, the Figure exuded a profound understanding that went beyond mere words—a language of imagination that spoke to the soul in a universally inspiring way.

The Figure's hair, a flowing stream of glistening celestial fiber wool, appeared to be intricately crafted with strands of aspirations. Every strand seemed to come alive, carrying the echoes of artistic pursuits and revealing the untold stories and unfulfilled dreams. It had a fluidity reminiscent of a flowing river, seamlessly connecting the individual to the vast and boundless realm of artistic expression.

The flowing locks seem to mimic the beauty of the cosmos, as if they hold the universe's secrets within. Every lock exudes a sense of mystery, as if it holds the secrets of the universe within its delicate yarns.

The celestial being's hair dances in perfect harmony with the cosmic symphony. Stars shimmer and dance within the strands, capturing the brilliance of countless suns. The strands have a mesmerising quality, as if they soak up the surrounding light and emit a mysterious glow that is both enchanting and ethereal.

Just like an artist's brushstrokes on a canvas, the being's cosmic tendrils extend, unveiling the hidden depths of its dark hair, exposing the infinite expanse of space contained within. In the ethereal strands of the divine entity's hair, tiny galaxies bloom, brimming with the vibrant essence of creation. In this vast expanse of the universe, new stars are born and old ones fade away, planets move in a graceful dance, and beautiful nebulae create a timeless masterpiece. The intricate patterns of the Figure's hair reflect the profound essence of the universe.

A radiant symbol adorned their forehead, emanating a mystical luminescence.

It appeared to represent the merging of creativity and actualization, a connection that bridged the worlds of fantasy and truth. This pulse resonated with the rhythm of artistic expression, emitting waves of inspiration that infused the very fabric of the imagination.

The Figure's clothing was like a living canvas, decorated with patterns that reflected the tales of artists from different cultures and time periods. Every symbol appeared to capture the very essence of a unique artistic voyage, weaving together an intricate pattern of interconnected stories. It felt as though the Figure encapsulated the essence of those who dared to dream through art.

The clothing reflected the vivid colours of Lesedi's most vibrant creations as if the spirit of his art had manifested into their garments. Every stride the Figure made left a shimmering trail in their wake, creating an unseen pathway that connected the mundane and the extraordinary, a testament to their otherworldly roots. Their flowing attire, a mesmerising blend of celestial colours, appeared to be crafted from the very fabric of existence. Flowing gracefully around them, the fabric softly murmured tales of far-off galaxies and the creation of celestial bodies. Just like an artist's brushstrokes on a canvas, the celestial being's aura danced and reshaped forming a mesmerising symphony of colours. The colours surpassed the boundaries of human understanding, surpassing earthly shades and mirroring the hidden marvels of the cosmos.

The Figure possessed a graceful form.

Their skin had a subtle shimmer, reminiscent of the moon's gentle reflection on a calm pond. The radiance that emanated from their very essence was a breathtaking array of hues, surpassing the confines of ordinary earthly colours. It felt as though they possessed the combined brilliance of every artist who had ever painted beneath the glow of the moon. This soft glow unveiled the delicate designs engraved on their skin, evoking memories of age-old star maps that traced the cosmic fabric. It felt like the universe itself had selected this form to reveal its exquisite beauty.

As Lesedi observed the Figure, a silent bond emerged, weaving their fates together like threads in a complex tapestry. The

Figure, with an extended hand, pointed towards the radiant dreams that enveloped them – scenes brought to life with the enchanting power of the paintbrush.

As they wandered through this enchanting realm, the individual started to uncover the mysteries of the enchanted paintbrush. Every brushstroke held a profound significance, transcending the physical realm and connecting with the ethereal. The Figure narrated how the brush had travelled through different dimensions, gathering bits of inspiration from various forms of artistic expression throughout the cosmos.

"Your brush," the Figure spoke, their words filled with a profound sense of wonder, "is a vessel for the stories of the universe. It has absorbed the colours of faraway galaxies, the echoes of tales long forgotten, and the whispers of artists who, like you, yearned to capture the indescribable. Within its bristles, you embrace the heritage of creators who moved with the cosmos."

Lesedi listened attentively, fully immersing himself in the profound revelation.

The streets of his hometown now appeared as a mere intersection in the vast labyrinth of life. The mysterious presence continued to lead him, revealing the boundless beauty of the world that surpassed anything he could have ever imagined.

"Every brushstroke," the Figure gestured to the ethereal dreams that enveloped them,

"is a profound conversation with the universe. Your art transcends the boundaries of this world; it resonates in the vast cosmic expanse. When you paint a picture of hope, the stars above join in a celestial chorus. When you depict the challenges faced by your community, it echoes through the cosmic vibrations. Your brush is not merely a tool; it is a narrator, a bridge between the visible and the invisible."

Lesedi, filled with wonder at the vastness of his artistic journey, was amazed by the limitless opportunities that lay ahead. Inspired by the enigmatic forces of the universe, the artist's creative process became a sacred bond with the cosmos, as every brushstroke forged a profound connection to the countless narratives reverberating throughout existence.

Lesedi, despite his initial doubts, couldn't resist the captivating aura emanating from the being. They seemed to embody the visions he dedicated to portraying in his artwork– a tangible proof of the profound impact of imagination.

"Who are you?" Lesedi's voice quivered with a blend of admiration and doubt.

In the realm of imagination, the enigmatic being spoke with a voice that seemed to float on the breeze. "I am a creator of worlds, a visionary who effortlessly moves between the familiar and the mysterious. Here, I am merely a companion, a wise presence guided by the power of your artistic expression."

As the speaker's words filled the space, an ethereal aura enveloped the surroundings, evoking a sense of cosmic wonder. Intrigued by the Figure's genuine words, Lesedi's initial scepticism began to fade, replaced by a growing sense of curiosity. The ethereal dreams that enveloped them throbbed with a cadence that mirrored the pulse of a cosmos brimming with creative possibilities.

"Your art has captivated the celestial fabric," the Figure continued, their eyes mirroring the vibrant array of colours that swirled in the dreamscape. "The brush you currently possess serves as a connection between different realms, a channel for stories that go beyond the limitations of time and space. It has chosen you to carry on the ageless practice of expressing the narratives that intertwine the fabric of life."

Lesedi, uncertain and bewildered by the strange encounter, paused before uttering another word. "But why me? What makes my art deserving of such... celestial recognition?"

The laughter of the Figure echoed softly, reminiscent of a gentle breeze. "Art transcends all boundaries, Lesedi. It has the power to speak with the deepest parts of our being, and your creations embody the rawness of life. Through your challenges, aspirations, and unwavering strength, the vastness of existence recognises a narrative that strikes a chord with the collective human experience. You possess the gift of storytelling, and your artistic medium serves as a gateway for the universe to manifest itself."

As the words of the Figure settled into the vast expanse of the dreamscape, Lesedi felt an intense shift within him. In his hand, the brush seemed to come alive with a newfound energy, as if aware of an intense shift within him too.

He remained skeptical, but the Figure remained determined, continuing to unveil the mysteries of the brush. They discussed worlds where emotions were tied to colours, where landscapes were shaped by a vivid imagination, and where every creation had a profound impact on the fabric of existence.

The radiant dreams seemed to have a life of their own, swirling gracefully around the Figure, reminiscent of the enchanting dance of fireflies in the night. Every dream contained a tale, a fragment of the individual's unique artistic odyssey that surpassed the boundaries of time and place.

He was captivated by the spectacle unfolding before him.

Doubts melted away, leaving behind a deep sense of purpose.

The mysterious Figure reached out with an enchanted paint-brush, captivating him. He felt a magnetic pull towards the brush, sensing the untapped potential that lay within his own creative spirit.

As Lesedi delicately brushed the canvas, a wave of inspiration washed over them, transporting them to a realm of ethereal dreams. The Figure smiled, radiating a sense of hope and the potential for profound change. United, they found themselves on the brink of a profound artistic journey, the bustling streets alive with the promise of hidden wonders yearning to be revealed.

Lesedi gazed intently at the Figure before him, torn between uncertainty and curiosity. He found himself torn between his doubts and an insatiable desire to explore.

"Why me?" he repeated, his voice filled with uncertainty.

In awe, he looked from the Figure to the paintbrush in his hand, its radiant glow a testament to the extraordinary power of his newfound artistic instrument.

"The brush has chosen you," whispered the Figure, their voice carried softly on the cosmic breeze, "and our purpose is to seek understanding."

The Figure's gaze, filled with profound knowledge, met Lesedi's, and an instant bond formed between them, as if guided by some cosmic force. It seemed as though the brush, a mystical creation from the universe's workshop, had sensed a special quality in Lesedi – something that went beyond the abilities of regular artists.

"Creativity," the Figure continued, "is a powerful energy that searches for channels. Your art is more than a mere reflection of your reality; it serves as a guiding light in the vast universe. The brush discovered you not by chance, but because your soul sings with the cosmic symphony. You possess the gift of storytelling, the ability to craft dreams, and have been chosen to move through the crossroads of different realms, infusing life into the very fabric of existence."

Lesedi, captivated by the profound mysteries of life, reflected on the vast interconnectedness of the universe that enveloped him. The words of the Figure resonated within the dreamscape, carrying the vibrant energy of artists from all corners of the cosmos. In perfect harmony with the universe, the brush became a vessel of his soul, pulsating with the energy of artistic expression.

"You see," the Figure gently urged, "your art is a profound conversation with the universe. The paintings you create, the narratives you tell—they reverberate through the fabric of reality. Your mission, aspiring artist, is to serve as a channel, a connection between the tangible and the ethereal. The brush chose you because the cosmos sensed the extraordinary power within you to mould fates with strokes of radiant imagination."

As they journeyed through the otherworldly landscapes, Lesedi's doubt diminished even more, giving way to a growing realisation of his part in the grand cosmic narrative. The brush's radiance grew stronger, echoing with the energy of a mission that surpassed the limits of his community and extended into the immense mysteries of the universe.

Together, they strolled, crafting tales that seamlessly merged with the essence of existence. He felt drawn to the radiant dreams he had witnessed and the captivating scenes he had painted, as if they were calling him to step into a new realm.

The atmosphere was charged with an unspoken exchange between Lesedi's uncertainties and the implicit potential of the mysterious Figure. The Figure's gaze, filled with profound knowledge, seemed to see right through Lesedi's doubts. It felt like the mysterious presence understood the deepest musings of the aspiring artist, recognising the doubts that burdened him and encouraging him to embrace the enchantment that lay within.

As the Figure continued their captivating tale, the ethereal radiance of the brush pulsed in sync with the emotions swirling within Lesedi. It felt as though the ethereal visions depicted in his paintings were springing into existence, gracefully moving to the enchanting rhythm of a mystical realm.

Lesedi, captivated, hung on every word as the mysterious Figure revealed the enigmatic origins and immense power of the brush. Every revelation seemed to be a stroke of brilliance, adding depth and meaning to his understanding, creating a narrative that went beyond what he had previously known.

The words of the Figure were more than just a tale; they served as a connection between realms, a reminder of the profound unity that exists in everything.

"The Luminae," the Figure described, "were ancient beings crafted from the fabric of creativity and imagination. They thrived in a world where ideas flowed effortlessly, unbound by the limitations of the physical realm. The magical paintbrush served as a powerful tool for artists to access an endless well-spring of inspiration. The brush seemed to have a mysterious origin as if it had been born from the shared dreams and ambitions of countless artists who had come before. It resonated with the echoes of their narratives, the emotions woven into their brushstrokes, and the insights gleaned from their artistic odysseys. It was a precious relic, handed down by those who had the courage to dream and envision."

As the Figure spoke, the radiant glow of the brush appeared to grow stronger, creating beautiful patterns of light that reflected the depth of the artistic soul. "It wasn't merely a tool, but rather a vessel of shared creativity, a guiding light that united artists throughout the tapestry of existence."

Lesedi, deeply moved by this revelation, experienced a strong sense of purpose and responsibility. He was chosen by the Luminae, just like the Figure, to carry on the tradition of artistic discovery. The brush beckoned him to join a mystical dance of creation, where each stroke had the power to mould not just his own world, but also the interconnected realms beyond.

The story told by the Figure intertwined the strands of inspiration, historical context, and the enigmatic power flowing from the paintbrush. It was a tale that spoke of boundless potential, of a fate entwined with the realm of Luminae. As the story unravelled, Lesedi felt that his artistic exploration was no longer limited to the streets of his township; it was a spiritual quest into the limitless realms of imagination that extended beyond boundaries.

Lesedi remained sceptical, despite being captivated by the Figure's impressive abilities. Instead, they turned it into a careful interest. He longed to grasp the meaning behind the brush, the Figure's relationship to it, and the part he was destined to fulfil in this enchanting tale.

In a world unbound by the constraints of time, where the very fabric of existence swayed in a celestial dance, the Luminae were born. They possessed a transcendent brilliance, serving as guardians of the cosmic tapestry, intricately entwining narratives into the very essence of existence. The tapestry they crafted extended beyond boundaries, a complex collage of life guided by the artist's hand.

This extraordinary creation, crafted by the Luminae's skilled hands, was far from ordinary. It radiated with the spirit of imagination, a vibrant manifestation of the Luminae's artistic brilliance. They soared beyond the confines of ordinary reality, navigating the intricate tapestry of life with the skill of celestial artisans.

The Luminae transcended the confines of mortal realms. They had the ability to dance among the stars, paint with the hues of galaxies, and shape the very essence of reality to their artistic desires. The brush, a testament to their skill, represented the connection between the physical and the spiritual, a conduit for the Luminae's celestial muse.

Every stroke of the Luminae's brush reverberated throughout the boundless expanse of creation, an exquisite harmony of hues and forms that shaped the very fabric of the cosmos. Every aspect of reality, from the birth of stars to the gentle winds that caress enchanted forests, was touched by the Luminae's artistic hand.

They possessed a profound understanding of the intricate harmony between creation and existence, akin to the wisdom of a revered sage. The Luminae were keen observers of the ebb and flow of cosmic energies, their every stroke intricately shaping destinies and infusing the cosmos with vibrant life. With the skill of a master artist, the brush effortlessly transcended boundaries, bridging the gap between the tangible and the mysterious.

In their world, time existed as a tapestry woven with boundless possibilities, not constrained by a linear thread. The Luminae revelled in the timeless symphony of creation, with the brush as their guiding baton, conducting the celestial ballet of existence.

And so the Luminae bestowed the enchanted brush upon artists throughout the ages, seeking those who could harmonise with the melody of creation. Lesedi, now immersed in this ethereal tale, could feel the profound impact of the Luminae's artistic expression resonating deep within him. He stood at the threshold of a bridge that connected different realms, beckoning him to enter a celestial workshop where his creativity would shape fresh narratives within the vast fabric of reality.

They had the remarkable talent to navigate through the intricate web of existence and shape the fundamental nature of the world. The brush, a remarkable creation, acted as a conduit connecting different realms. The character portrayed the Luminae as otherworldly creatures, radiating with the colours of imagination. Art was not a separate entity but an integral part of life's symphony.

The brush, infused with the spirit of the Luminae's shared imagination, transformed into a potent talisman. It chose artists from different realms, whose souls beat to the cadence of undiscovered narratives and unexplored aspirations.

This enchanting brush possessed a power that surpassed its physical form; it served as a vessel for the Luminae's boundless imagination. It possessed a remarkable talent for sensing the pulsating hearts of artists across different realms, searching for those whose spirits harmonised with the cadence of untold tales and unexplored aspirations.

In their infinite wisdom, the Luminae understood that the true power of the brush resided not only in its otherworldly bristles but in the artists it favoured. The essence of the Luminae, intricately entwined within the brush's very fibres, possessed a natural intelligence. It had a keen understanding of the silent dialect of fervour, resolve, and artistic inspiration that blazed within the soul of an artist.

As the Luminae passed down this mystical artifact through the corridors of time, it sought out individuals who, similar to Lesedi, found themselves at the crossroads of fate and longing.

Those who aspire to create vibrant worlds with the power of their imagination resonate with the Luminae's deep desire for boundless creativity.

This selection process was not random; it was a harmonious symphony, a dance of fate where the brush selected its wielder with a profound sense of purpose. It attracted those who dared to dream beyond the limitations of their everyday lives, people whose creativity would serve as a connection between different worlds.

In the moment when the brush landed in Lesedi's hands, it carried a deeper meaning than just the transfer of an object. It symbolised the recognition of his innate artistic talent. Lesedi felt a deep connection as the Luminae's essence flowed through the bristles, creating a profound bond between artist and tool.

As Lesedi grasped the brush, he embraced the profound responsibility of preserving the Luminae's rich heritage, entrusted with the sacred mission of imbuing the physical realm with the enchantment of his creative vision. Inspired by the ethereal beauty of the Luminae, their artistry has found a way to transcend the boundaries of time and space, leaving an everlasting legacy. Inspired by the enchanting whispers of the universe, Lesedi's brush held the power to bring forth radiant dreams onto his canvas.

In the story, the Luminae, enigmatic beings of light and imagination, had a crucial part to play. These otherworldly beings perceived the deep longing within the individual's soul. It was a longing to unite the physical and the metaphysical, a yearning to transcend the boundaries of the present and embrace the possibilities of the future.

The Figure described a time when the Luminae had emerged, their arrival a captivating display of light and movement. With a mixture of excitement and caution, the individual had taken hold of the enchanted paintbrush, a gateway to the realm of Luminae. It was an invitation to explore a world beyond the ordinary, where imagination shaped the fabric of reality.

The Figure effortlessly transcended the ordinary, immersing themselves in a world of boundless potential as they connected with the Luminae. The character depicted the initial brush-stroke, a movement that sparked a cascade of transformative vitality. The streets came alive with vibrant colours, as if they were flowing rivers of light. The buildings stood tall, showcasing an incredible display of artistic brilliance.

As Lesedi delved into each story of artistic exploration, he couldn't help but feel a deep connection to his own personal journey. The Luminae detected a presence within him, much like they did with the Figure. It was a profound connection that went beyond the limitations of time and space, uniting artists across different dimensions.

As the Figure's story unravelled, Lesedi started to grasp the Luminae's role as more than just distant overseers, but rather as active participants in the magnificent creation. Their mesmerising display of brilliance seemed to beckon, recognising that the beauty of art transcends boundaries and unites beings from all corners of the universe.

Immersed in a realm of infinite creativity, the individual had unlocked the profound essence of the brush. It served as a conduit between realms, a medium for artists to connect, express, and ignite inspiration. The Luminae's gift went beyond the mere magic within the brush. It was a profound realisation that art possessed the ability to surpass the boundaries of individual existence.

Lesedi, in a state of wonder, reflected on the Luminae's impact on his artistic journey.

Inspired by the enchanting world of Luminae, the paintbrush possessed a mystical power that transcended ordinary tools. It held the ability to reveal the hidden wonders of a realm where art seamlessly merged with the fabric of existence.

This realm, as the Figure elucidated, resided within the spaces that lie between worlds, the ethereal junctures where the boundaries of dreams and reality intertwine. It was a place where the ordinary turned into something magical, and every artist became a creator of fate.

As the Figure spoke, Lesedi could envision the intricate tapestry of existence, where the threads of the universe intertwined. Just like a master artist, the brush unlocks the door to a celestial atelier, where inspiration flows from personal experiences and the shared consciousness of the Luminae.

The story captivated him with its sense of awe and duty. They had explored different worlds, brought new worlds to life, and unleashed the hidden power within the paintbrush. However, this journey lacked fulfilment without a deserving heir, someone capable of carrying the brush's legacy into the next phase of cosmic creation.

Lesedi, deeply moved by this profound realisation, was burdened by the immense expectations of the Luminae. As if touched by the divine, he was chosen as the next guardian of the brush.

The Figure's history unravelled like a masterpiece crafted with elements of enchantment and ingenuity. In a distant realm that transcended Lesedi's comprehension, the individual was once a creative soul wrestling with uncertainties, much akin to Lesedi's own struggles. They discussed a realm where the lines between fantasy and reality were flexible, a realm where creators possessed the power to mould the very fabric of life.

The Figure's initial experiences with the brush were filled with doubt and hesitation.

Similar to Lesedi, they had doubts about the genuineness of this enchanting instrument. However, as they cautiously started to discover its potential, the ordinary streets of their own world turned into radiant landscapes.

In the realm of artistry, the brush transcended its utilitarian purpose and became a wellspring of limitless imagination. They had the ability to create vivid images that were both awe-inspiring and deeply meaningful. The illustration showcased the brush's ability to craft intricate worlds, capturing the depth of emotions and untold stories.

Their journey exemplified the power of the brush to bring about profound change.

The artist, who was once sceptical, transformed into a visionary, utilising a magical tool to bring about growth and ignite inspiration in others. Every brushstroke was a testament to the artist's skill and their talent for bringing dreams to life.

The world of the Figure, previously limited by the mundane, now throbbed with the exceptional. They discussed the power of art to transcend boundaries and unite people from different realms. It appeared that the brush was a divine offering for artists to transcend the boundaries of mere depiction and enter the realm of artistic creation.

Lesedi, captivated by the Figure's storytelling, was transported to a realm where dreams and truth intertwined seamlessly. The brush held within it the power to transform, a living testament to the limitless possibilities that lay ahead. After hearing the Figure's captivating tale, Lesedi was filled with a sense of wonder and inspiration, ready to set off on his own artistic adventure.

The Figure, emanating an ethereal glow, reached out with a mystical brush towards Lesedi, their intentions filled with solemnity. "Your affinity for the brush is not a mere coincidence, young artist," the Figure declared, their voice exuding a soothing yet authoritative aura in the room. "It has chosen you, and with it arrives a duty—one that surpasses the limits of your comprehension."

Lesedi experienced a mix of excitement and uncertainty as he tried to make sense of the extraordinary encounter. You possess a unique ability to create captivating art that goes beyond mere representation. Your work has the power to inspire change and ignite growth. The brush effortlessly captures the connection between your soul and the limitless possibilities it holds.

The Figure continued to share their personal experience of doubt and exploration, recalling how they, too, had questioned the enigmatic essence of the brush. Yet, with the help of wise mentors, they had mastered the art of exploring the boundless horizons it presented. "This goes beyond mere artistry, Lesedi. It delves into the profound depths of creation and its profound influence on the world that surrounds us."

As the Figure spoke, the space seemed to undergo a remarkable transformation. The architecture was transformed into a mesmerising tapestry, unveiling scenes of awe-inspiring beauty and countless untold tales. The speaker's words carried a profound sense of wisdom that seemed to go beyond time, captivating Lesedi with stories of artists who had risen above the mundane.

"You are not alone in this journey," the Figure reassured, their gaze penetrating through the doubts that filled Lesedi's mind. "I am here to be your guiding light, to mentor you in the art of unleashing your inner potential. Together, we will explore the realms of creativity, where the ordinary transforms into something extraordinary."

Lesedi's doubts slowly transformed into a deep sense of determination. The mentor's guidance went beyond mere advice; it was an invitation to a world where art became a profound expression of the essence of life. His voice filled the mystical chamber as he confidently and humbly declared, "I accept." The words lingered in the air, carrying a profound promise that transcended the ordinary.

As he spoke, the Figure's eyes sparkled with admiration. The mentorship was more than just a transfer of knowledge; it was a profound agreement, a dedication to a lineage of artists who had tapped into the incredible potential of the magical brush.

The environment was filled with an electric energy, as every-one eagerly awaited the artistic adventure that lay ahead - a journey that would come to life on the canvas of reality.

At that moment, the brush became a bridge between realms, pulsating with a power that echoed the rhythm of Lesedi's heart. It felt like a manifestation of a timeless and boundless legacy. In the ethereal light, the enigmatic presence emerged as a guiding force, protecting the radiant aspirations that ignited the minds of artists throughout time.

The Figure's next words resonated in the chamber, each syllable filled with deep artistic insight. "In embracing this path, you are not only connected to the rich legacy of artists who came before you. The ethereal visions you bring to life will leave a lasting imprint on the tapestry of human experience. Your art will serve as a conduit, bridging the tangible and intangible, the familiar and the mysterious."

Lesedi, inspired by the unfolding revelation, felt a strong

sense of determination welling up within him. The mentorship was a commitment to embrace the spirit of imagination and meaning. As he grasped the brush, the ethereal dreams murmured softly, unveiling fragments of untold tales. He embodied the true spirit of artistic heritage. The passing of the tool was more than just a simple exchange; it represented an essential transfer of energy, connecting Lesedi to a long line of influential artists who have left their mark on the world.

As Lesedi entered the chamber, a sense of enchantment filled the air, enveloping him in a luminous aura that seemed to transport him to another realm. Like the great masters of art before, Lesedi embarked on a mentorship that would take him on a journey beyond the limits of his imagination. With the brush as his guide and the Figure as his inspiration, he was ready to embark on an artistic odyssey.

After the Figure finished their revelation, the space seemed to vibrate with an ethereal energy. Lesedi found himself grappling with a mix of excitement and trepidation as he processed the revelations that had been laid bare before him. The atmosphere seemed to vibrate with the potential of something that lay beyond his understanding.

The ethereal visions on his paintings appeared to resonate with the enigmatic strokes of the artist's brush. At that moment, Lesedi found himself on the verge of an incredible journey, a path that extended into uncharted territory.

He seemed to have a deep connection with the essence of creativity.

Enveloped in a mesmerising tapestry of ethereal threads, he found himself intricately linked to a mysterious presence, a realm of enchantment, and a world brimming with limitless potential.

In the stillness that ensued, the mysterious presence disappeared, leaving Lesedi to navigate the boundless realm of artistic inspiration. Inspired by the enchanting world of imagination, the dreamscape now thrived with a vibrant vitality, echoing the ethereal essence of artistic expression. The ethereal visions on his paintings appeared to dance with a vibrant energy, as if they had absorbed the insights of the subject and now possessed a profound significance.

Lost in this vast and otherworldly expanse, Lesedi felt a delicate change in the air.

It felt like the atmosphere was alive with the vibrations of imagination, revealing enigmatic truths that only he could grasp. The words of the Figure resonated in his thoughts, leading him toward unexplored territories of artistic discovery.

His artistic soul took flight.

The doubts that were once silenced have now been overshadowed by a symphony of vibrant dreams. Just like an artist with boundless creativity, he saw endless potential in every shade and turned empty canvases into vibrant worlds.

The departure of the Figure signified not the end, but rather the start of a new journey—a gateway to the profound secrets of the paintbrush and the boundless possibilities it possessed. Inspired by the spirit of adventure, Lesedi eagerly delved into the depths of his imagination, where the dreamscape beckoned with endless possibilities.

In this ethereal realm where the boundaries of time and reality converge, Lesedi emerged as a vessel bridging the gap between different dimensions. He stood poised to capture the radiant visions that called out to him, leading him towards a fate intricately woven with the strands of enchantment and artistic expression.

The radiant visions in his paintings transcended the realm of mere pictures, opening gateways to unexplored realms. Every stroke of the brush opened doors to limitless worlds of imagination. Lesedi stood at the threshold of this artistic tapestry, poised to spin tales that surpassed the boundaries of the everyday world.

Just like an artist deeply connected to their craft, Lesedi's brush became an extension of his being, effortlessly merging with the cosmic energies that surrounded him. It felt as though the universe itself recognised the merging of artist and instrument, a beautiful union that surpassed the mundane.

As Lesedi made his silent vow to embrace the unknown, he felt a wave of inspiration flowing through him. The brush in his hand was more than just a tool. It served as a gateway to the infinite realms of creativity. Every brushstroke became a profound connection with the cosmos, a graceful intertwining of the artist's spirit and the enigmas of existence.

As Lesedi embarked on his artistic journey, he found a new dimension with the brush as his guide. His paintings captured ethereal scenes that reflected the vastness of the universe, where celestial bodies danced gracefully across the dark expanse. Inspired by the enchanting world of his thoughts, the ethereal visions came to life with a vibrant intensity that transcended the boundaries of the ordinary.

The transformative journey beckoned to him like a blank canvas, ready to be transformed into a masterpiece. Lesedi effortlessly moved through the ethereal realm of his own making, every stroke of his brush imbuing his creations with a touch of enchantment, bringing them to life. Lesedi, the artist with a deep sense of humility, stood at the crossroads of imagination and reality, his unwavering commitment resounding through the vast realms of his artistic exploration.

Chapter 7: The Artistic Odyssey

In the serene atmosphere of the studio, where ethereal visions seemed to linger like whispers of untold stories, Lesedi immersed himself in a realm that transcended conventional tools of art. In the realm of art, a mysterious painter emerged as a guide and confidant, leading the way through the ethereal realms that brought the enchanted paintbrush to life.

Their teachings were conveyed through a language that went beyond conventional understanding, a silent conversation between the artist and their brush, a connection that reached deep into the depths of the soul. The mysterious artist unveiled hidden truths written in the constellations, communicating the universal language with Lesedi. Every brushstroke, guided by an ethereal wisdom, weaved tales that defied the limits of perception—a graceful interplay with the cosmic forces that unite our world.

In tune with the universe's mysteries, Lesedi's brush danced across the canvas, channelling the cosmic energies that give rise to galaxies and nebulae. In the realm of artistic expression, the painter's words were unspoken, yet Lesedi absorbed them with a deep understanding that grew with each radiant brushstroke.

The training went beyond just technique; it focused on being in tune with the cosmic rhythms. Lesedi developed a deep sensitivity to the subtle movements of unseen forces, attuned his ears to the harmonies of the cosmos, and skillfully turned them into tangible works of art. Inspired by the enchantment of the universe, the brush effortlessly made celestial whispers and cosmic winds into strokes that brought forth unimaginable wonders.

In that hallowed realm where the boundary between the tangible and the intangible was delicate, Lesedi unearthed the realisation that artistic expression went past the bounds of traditional mediums and delved into the unexplored depths of the human spirit. Inspired by the enigmatic painter, Lesedi's artistic voice soared beyond the boundaries of mortal comprehension, taking us on a cosmic odyssey.

In the sacred stillness of creative connection, Lesedi's artistic journey unfurled—a harmonious blend of energies, a graceful expression of celestial muse, and a gateway into the enigmatic realms unlocked by the mystical paintbrush.

Lesedi's hands became conduits of ethereal forces, much like a vessel for cosmic wisdom. He was encouraged to look beyond the surface of ordinary perception. His control over the enchanted paintbrush became a mesmerising symphony of intertwined forces.

Guided by the enigmatic painter, Lesedi discovered a deep connection between the brush and the infinite wellspring of universal inspiration. With a touch of enchantment, the ethereal visions on Lesedi's canvases became captivating tales that stirred the soul.

The strokes, once hesitant, now exude confidence as they capture the ethereal dance of the cosmos and the secrets whispered by distant galaxies. Lesedi's hands, guided by an ethereal power, created vivid scenes that went beyond the limits of human imagination. The radiant dreams burst forth with vivid vitality, weaving stories of hidden realms, unexperienced emotions, and the extraordinary made tangible.

Lesedi explored the depths of his art, uncovering fundamental lessons that couldn't be learned in traditional art studios. It felt like experiencing the infinite beauty of the universe—the enchanting whispers of stardust, the harmonious flow of invisible forces, and the grandeur of celestial melodies.

The training pushed the limits of his physical and mental abilities.

His artistic expression ventured beyond the familiar, delving into the realm of the metaphysical. His brushstrokes brought forth narratives that reverberated not only on the canvas but within the very essence of life itself.

The radiant dreams now served as evidence of a strong connection with mysterious powers. Lesedi's journey, guided by a mysterious artist, was a significant experience—an unfolding of the remarkable potential hidden within the simple act of painting.

In the realm of artistic evolution, challenges have always been present, sometimes appearing as obstacles and other times as opportunities for growth. Inspired by the enigmatic painter,

Lesedi was faced with the challenge of creating something truly extraordinary. At first, the canvas captured Lesedi's inner turmoil—a blend of uncertainty, indecision, and the heavy burden of his own constraints.

He faced a challenging task, and the canvas became a testament to his determination.

The initial hundred attempts resounded with a sense of self-doubt. The colours on the canvas lacked the vibrancy of his vision; the brushstrokes fell short in capturing the essence of bridging reality with the impossible. He found himself facing perplexing obstacles that seemed to mock his abilities and amplify his lack of confidence.

He struggled to grasp the elusive power of the brush, feeling trapped by his own limited perception. His mind was ensnared in a labyrinth of self-doubt, hindering his pursuit of greatness. The dreams that once radiated with brilliance now wavered hesitantly, mirroring the inner turmoil.

In the dance of dreams and uncertainty, Lesedi found himself faltering, pausing on the edge of the unfamiliar. Painting the impossible was a formidable task, a canvas that stretched across the vast expanse of his uncertainties. He found himself trapped in the familiar embrace of his comfort zone, unable to escape its powerful hold.

The ethereal dreams that once burned brightly now seemed to waver, overshadowed by the uncertainties that plagued the mind. In the realm of artistic creation, where a mysterious painter served as his patient guide, Lesedi's brushstrokes were cautious, as if bound by the weight of his own boundaries.

He was drawn to the enchanting melodies that resonated throughout the cosmos, but they always seemed to elude his grasp. He longed to create a masterpiece, yet the notes of fear and doubt resonated more strongly in his thoughts.

With a deep understanding, the mysterious artist silently observed, perceiving the inner turmoil within Lesedi's soul. The universe's brush, vibrating with boundless possibilities, eagerly anticipated the gentle caress that would reveal its hidden wisdom. Yet, Lesedi's hand quivered on the edge of the unimaginable, ensnared by the weight of uncertainty.

It felt like embarking on a profound expedition into the vast expanse of creativity, where unexplored realms of imagination collided with the gravitational pull of the familiar. In these moments of uncertainty, Lesedi faced his inner demons, struggling with the uncertainties that threatened to hold him back from embracing a more extraordinary life.

Their gaze reminiscent of the stars, their communication surpassed words and instead spoke through the ethereal language of cosmic energies. The hundred attempts were not failures, but rather steps in the cosmic dance, each stumble a movement towards the crescendo of artistic liberation. The brush eagerly anticipated the moment when Lesedi's strokes would turn the familiar canvas into a realm of boundless imagination.

In the depths of his introspection, Lesedi was privy to the mysterious whispers of the unattainable, "Lesedi, my student, there is a hidden world waiting to be discovered in the depths of your thoughts—a blank canvas where endless possibilities await your artistic expression."

Lesedi paused, brush in hand, stared at the blank canvas, "Is it really impossible? What mysteries are concealed within this puzzle?"

With a wise grin, the Figure answered, "The realm of impossibility is not something imposed upon us, but rather a reflection of the limits we place on our own beliefs. It pushes the boundaries of your abilities, revealing the hidden barriers you've unconsciously set for yourself."

"Just as an acclaimed author captures the essence of life through their words, I just have to depict the challenges and aspirations of my community, the vibrant dreams that thrive within the township," Lesedi said firmly.

The Figure chuckled, "Quite the challenge, Lesedi. It's an invitation to expand your artistic horizons, to create not just pictures but stories that go beyond the ordinary."

Lesedi stared at the empty canvas, "Where do I even start?"

With a knowing glimmer, "Start by understanding that the impossible is not something outside of yourself that is working against you. It's a journey that beckons you to surpass your perceived limits."

Lesedi inhaling deeply, "So, an inner journey, huh?"

"A journey that transcends the boundaries of the cosmos. The impossible is a powerful energy, constantly evolving alongside the beat of your growth as an individual. Imagine it not as a distant desire, but as a close companion in the dance of bringing something into existence." The Figure answered

Wearing the burden of possibility, "So, the transformation is more important than the canvas?"

"Embracing the unknown is a transformative experience, where uncertainties dissolve and reveal the fiery essence of your capabilities. Do not be afraid of it, Lesedi, for the rebirth of your artistic soul rests inside the challenge that it presents."

In his humble studio, Lesedi faced the cosmic brush with a mix of excitement and nervousness. The strokes that used to flow effortlessly across his canvas have changed into elusive patterns, slipping through his fingers like fleeting dreams. The ethereal harmony that reverberated through the enchanted strands appeared to taunt him, a constant reminder of the limits he struggled to comprehend.

Every endeavour to capture the unattainable resulted in periods of exasperation and uncertainty. The canvas evolved into a fierce arena where Lesedi wrestled not only with the celestial brush, but also with the inner darkness that resided within him. In the midst of his artistic struggle, insecurities whispered in the silence, casting doubts like lurking spectres.

Lesedi frowning, brush in hand, "Why am I unable to paint it? What is preventing me from moving forward?"

The celestial brush stayed quiet, its otherworldly radiance unaltered. It longed for the touch of a visionary who could surpass the boundaries of conventional thought.

Lesedi found himself in a constant battle, questioning the very essence of his artistic being. He felt as if he were an astronomer, gazing at the cosmos, unable to grasp the immense expanse of the unexplored territories. Many times he immersed the brush into vivid pigments, only to see them crumble into discordant chaos on the canvas.

Self-doubt creeps into Lesedi's mind, whispering its insidious message. "You are not meant for the impossible. Stay within your area of expertise."

However, amidst his uncertainties, a spark of unwavering resolve glimmered. Lesedi, driven by an unwavering determination, persevered. Every setback transformed into a building block, and every effort bore the burden of his growing comprehension. He wrestled not only with the vast expanse of the universe but also with the intangible restraints that confined his artistic expression.

Lesedi muttered to himself, "There's a hidden truth eluding

me. Discovering the path to conquer the unimaginable."

In the vast expanse of the universe, a brush of destiny patiently awaited the perfect moment for Lesedi to uncover the enigmatic truth hidden within his soul. The struggle went beyond the strokes on the canvas, becoming a cosmic dance with the shadows. It was an exploration of the self that transcended the realm of visible artistry.

In this realm of creative energy, Lesedi was not just capturing scenes; he was moulding his own metamorphosis. Immersed in the realm of infinite possibilities, the ethereal brush gently unveiled the hidden truths that yearned to be discovered. Embracing the impossible was not a challenge to be conquered; rather, it was a frontier to be embraced from within. And thus, the battle persisted, every brushstroke a testament to the ever-changing symphony of Lesedi's artistic soul.

Lost in his own thoughts, Lesedi found himself surrounded by the remnants of his creative endeavours. The canvas before him reflected the tumultuous chaos he had brought to life. Lost in deep thought, he furrowed his brow, reflecting on the question that reverberated within the depths of his consciousness: "What did the concept of the impossible signify to him?"

Whispering to himself, "The impossible... It's not merely about surpassing my current abilities. It's all about pushing the limits I've unconsciously imposed on myself. It's as if I'm attempting to comprehend the vastness of the cosmos, yet grasping its true meaning remains elusive."

He came to the realisation that what seemed impossible was merely a reflection of the limitations he had placed upon himself. It was like looking into a mirror that showed his doubts and fears, which had become deeply ingrained in his artistic identity. It wasn't just about capturing extraordinary scenes on canvas; it was a personal quest to uncover the enigmas within.

Examining the untidy canvas, "Each brushstroke that dissolves into disorder serves as a gentle nudge, urging me to explore further depths, not only in the realm of art but also within my own being. Embracing the unknown is a realm of endless possibilities, just waiting to be discovered."

Lesedi came to the realisation that what seemed impossible was not the end, but rather a new beginning. It was an invitation to go beyond the confines of familiar thinking and embrace the unknown that lies beyond. In his artwork, he captured a dissonance that mirrored the inner conflict he experienced— a constant struggle between his hesitant self and the aspiring artist within him.

With unwavering resolve, "If I can truly grasp the essence of what seems unattainable, I will discover the path to bring it to life through my art. It's not only about scenes or images; it's about liberating oneself from uncertainty and embracing the limitless possibilities that reside within."

Like a masterful composer, the cacophony of conflicting thoughts suddenly harmonised into a beautiful arrangement of endless potential. Lesedi, with a newfound grasp of the unfathomable, readied himself to face the vast expanse once again. The struggle was not merely an artistic obstacle, but rather a profound voyage of self-discovery, delving into the boundless horizons that beckoned his creative soul.

Immersed in the seclusion of his studio, encircled by the remnants of his endeavours to overcome the insurmountable, Lesedi's contemplation grew more profound. In his mind, he could still hear the echoes of his struggles—the hurtful words from his stepfather, the heavy burden of expectations, and the constant presence of poverty that had moulded his reality.

Whispering to himself, "It's more than just the tools and the images I'm striving to bring to life. It revolves around me. I've been preoccupied with the external challenges, the hardships, the societal pressures... Yet, the true struggle lies deep within."

As he explored the depths of his own fears, Lesedi made a profound discovery. He was apprehensive about achieving success, not because of the act of painting the impossible, but because of the potential consequences that would follow. The idea of surpassing his present situation filled him with fear. Deep within, he came to the realisation that achieving success required venturing into unknown territories, leaving behind the familiar struggles of the past.

Reflectively, Lesedi thought to himself, "I've been hesitant, afraid of the very thing I desire. I have a deep fear of achieving success. Success would entail entering what I've always envisioned—a life free from never-ending struggle. Embracing the unknown can be a daunting prospect, as it challenges us to step outside our comfort zones. Yet, it is through these struggles that we find growth and transformation."

The revelation lingered in the air, burdened by the weight of personal exploration.

Lesedi's artistic journey had transformed into a powerful symbol of his quest to confront the inner obstacles that imprisoned him. Inspired by the great masters of the arts, he gazed upon the cosmic brush, a tool that held the power to unlock boundless potential and transcend the limitations of a life plagued by poverty.

Yet, the artist knew that overcoming the fear of the unknown and the fear of success was a crucial obstacle to overcome. This cosmic brush has become a powerful instrument in breaking down the barriers of fear and self-doubt.

With a resolute look, "Creating art that defies expectations goes beyond mere subjects; it's about overcoming the inner doubts. It's about embracing a life that goes beyond struggle. Perhaps the true test lies not in the brush, but in confronting the truth that I have been avoiding..."

Lesedi came to a deep realisation, that the boundaries of possibility were merely illusions waiting to be shattered. He embarked on a life-changing expedition, delving deep into the uncharted realms of his own mind. His art possessed a mesmerising quality, capable of connecting boundaries and reshaping his entire being. He felt compelled to face the fear that had kept him trapped in a life of scarcity and restrictions.

He longed to create more than just mere images, but to paint a masterpiece that would symbolise his personal freedom. He delved into the depths of his imagination, exploring the deep influence of artistic expression on his life.

In each precise stroke, Lesedi embarked on a profound journey, balancing the realms of possibility with the uncharted depths of his creative mind. He embraced the idea that what seemed impossible was not a rigid concept, but rather a fluid energy that reshaped as he continued to develop his artistic abilities. It was a masterpiece of colours that extended beyond what the eye could see, echoing with the ever-changing rhythm of his soul.

As Lesedi ventured further into the mysterious realm of artistic exploration, he discovered that what seemed impossible was not just a mere challenge, but a living entity that responded to the rhythm of his creative spirit. His paintings were filled with ethereal dreams, carrying viewers to a world where reality and imagination merged in a way never seen before.

He wholeheartedly embraced the idea that the most challenging situations can lead to profound personal growth. It served as a bridge, linking what was familiar to what was unfamiliar. He found that every brushstroke was a gateway to uncharted realms, a voyage unfolding with the limitless possibilities of his artistic vision. He embraced the notion that the impossible was not a fixed endpoint, but rather a constantly shifting horizon in his artistic journey.

Inspired by the enchanting visions and profound insights of a mysterious artist, Lesedi fearlessly embraced the mystical realm of the cosmic dance, where the realms of possibility and impossibility intertwined to reveal a captivating journey of artistic exploration.

As Lesedi immersed himself in this profound journey, the realm of the unimaginable changed into a hallowed sanctuary. Here, the flames of his uncertainty didn't consume him; instead, they turned into transformative fires, purifying the essence of his creative self. Creating a masterpiece, Lesedi experienced the incredible shift that turned his fears into courage and his uncertainties into clarity.

In the eyes of the enigmatic painter, Lesedi possessed a profound power, as if he were a chosen vessel of the universe. They fostered the fiery essence of his capabilities, urging him to confront his inner demons and find power in the very challenges that had once imprisoned him. The impossible transformed from an unconquerable obstacle into a gateway to self-discovery, revealing the profound depths of his creative spirit.

In this journey of self-exploration, Lesedi's art went through an immense change.

The paintings that once reflected his hardships have turned into gateways to worlds where creativity roamed unrestricted. As a result of combining uncertainty with resolve, his luminous visions took on forms and colours that went beyond his earlier creative pursuits.

As Lesedi delved into the profound wisdom of the mysterious painter In his artistic journey, the impossible became a constant companion, pushing him to explore the boundaries of his creativity. Once a terrifying place, Lesedi learnt to appreciate the crucible as a haven where he created art and a deep connection with the boundless potential inside himself.

In the crucible of life's challenges, Lesedi's artistic voice echoed with a melody that surpassed the ordinary notes of everyday existence. With the mysterious painter's guiding light, the cosmic brush gracefully moved over the canvas, creating symphonies that mirrored Lesedi's profound creative awakening. Inspired by the spirit of adventure and the pursuit of greatness, the once insurmountable obstacle now beckoned as an opportunity for something truly remarkable.

With every brushstroke, Lesedi experienced a profound transformation, as the limitations of the mundane world faded away. The glowing dreams, which were imbued with the alchemy of his struggles and desires, materialised as vivid hues that conveyed narratives that were beyond the scope of conventional comprehension. The seemingly insurmountable became an avenue of expression that linked Lesedi's creative spirit to the infinite possibilities of art.

In this hallowed place of creation, the crucible became a haven where Lesedi's artwork blossomed into a symbol of strength, optimism, and change. The glowing fantasies and cosmic symphony created by his brush were evidence of the boundless potential inside his creative spirit. He approached the impossible with a sense of curiosity and a desire to push the boundaries of his creativity.

With each touch of the cosmic brush, the painting turned into a beautiful tapestry of the ether. Lesedi's hand danced in perfect synchrony with the ethereal dreams, their vivid colours spinning stories that surpassed the boundaries of ordinary comprehension. In the depths of his past struggles, they now emerged as mere shadows beneath the vibrant hues, murmuring tales of strength and victory.

The impossible, which was once seen as an impenetrable obstacle, turned into a bridge that crossed the gap between the normal and the special. Reflecting the kaleidoscope of Lesedi's inner world, the luminous visions were produced from the alchemy of his hardships and desires. Every stroke of the brush became a pathway, a voyage that linked his artistic soul to the infinite possibilities of creative manifestation.

The painting became into a gateway to other worlds as the lines between the mundane blurred. Like echoes of a cosmic melody, the bright colours stirred up feelings and stories that didn't fit with what most people would think.

Lesedi found comfort in this higher level of art, not by running away from his problems, but by turning them into a colourful patchwork that spoke of hope, change, and the unbreakable spirit inside. The impossibility was no longer a barrier; rather, it was the precise medium through which Lesedi painted the luminous fantasies that were a part of his soul.

He went through a transformation that went beyond the sphere of artistic expression when he was being heated in the furnace of the impossible. He navigated through uncharted seas of his own potential, transforming struggles into stepping stones along the way. Every brushstroke was not just a mere mark on canvas, but a profound unveiling of the limitless universe within his soul.

The luminous visions, moulded by the combination of his hardships and ambitions, unfurled into a story of metamorphosis. It was a tale that unfolded not only through vivid scenes, but also through the very essence of the colours he skillfully employed. In the process of creating a symphony of colours that reflected the glowing visions of the unattainable, the cosmic brush, which had become an extension of his emancipated soul, danced over the canvas.

His artistic style found a home on this journey of change, and the problems that used to scare him now inspired his art. Painting became a way for him to grow as an artist and as a person. It captured the spirit of his change. Not only did the glowing dreams that were painted by the cosmic brush reflect the exterior beauty of his artwork, but they also represented the psychological victory over the constraints that he had put on himself.

In his pursuit to capture the unattainable on canvas, Lesedi unearthed the boundless depths of his artistic ingenuity. The mystical brush, once an enigmatic tool, became a trusted ally on the journey of self-exploration. The radiant dreams captured on the canvas were not only a display of his artistic talent, but also a testament to his bravery in embracing the seemingly impossible and turning it into a guiding light for his own potential.

Through the intricate dance that took place between the brush and the canvas, Lesedi came to understand the transformational power of perseverance. The things that he had previously written off as "failures" were really the catalysts for his most significant epiphanies. In the process of discarding each painting, he was able to see not just his own personal development but also the progression of his artistic soul.

He was able to cultivate the qualities of resiliency and determination by putting himself through a series of difficult experiences. The radiant aspirations that evaded him in the beginning now stood ready, gleaming with promise. He grasped the concept that this endeavour was not a short burst of energy, but rather a long and enduring exploration of his own artistic potential.

Once thought to be failures, the canvases he threw away became quiet witnesses to his perseverance. Every brushstroke, even the ones that didn't bring about the miraculous, served as a testament to his unwavering dedication to the journey of self-exploration. Lesedi understood that the real enchantment resided not only in the ultimate masterpiece, but in the journey of discovering the enigmas within himself.

With his newfound knowledge, he saw that the things he considered failures were really important stops along the way to becoming an artist.

Every endeavour was a stroke on the canvas of his personal development. It felt as though the glowing dreams, which were now more vivid than they had ever been, were praising his tenacity. He was led by a mystical force, a tool that presented both obstacles and enlightenment, as he navigated the intricate maze of uncertainty and eventually arrived at the shores of personal revelation.

The quest to capture the unattainable went beyond mere brushstroke expertise; it demanded a profound understanding of one's own inner self. Lesedi learnt the rhythm of his own strength through the ups and downs of his creative battles. This turned the canvas into not only a display of his artistic skill but also a live example of how persistence can change things.

As Lesedi explored the intricate tapestry of the universe, a deep understanding dawned upon him, unfolding gently like the delicate petals of a blooming flower. It was strange how the brush felt like an extension of his body. It changed from a tool to a way for him to express his feelings and thoughts, a way for the whispers in his soul to become stories that he could see and feel.

As he painted, he witnessed his unique artistic expression manifest from the depths of his creative mind. The radiant aspirations that once appeared far-off and out of reach were now within his grasp, intricately intertwined with the essence of his artwork. It used to be scary to think about the impossible, but now it was a fun place to explore and let his imagination run wild.

He had learnt to harness the cosmic energies, and the brush, directed by those forces, glided across the canvas with an easy elegance. It captured more than just scenes, it evoked emotions and told stories through its colours. Lesedi discovered that facing the seemingly impossible was not a hindrance, but rather an opportunity to explore the depths of his own comprehension and create something truly remarkable.

In his sacred space of creativity, Lesedi found himself surrounded by canvases that resonated with the ethereal visions of the unimaginable. He couldn't help but be in awe of the growth and transformation of his artistic voyage. Once a mysterious instrument, the brush had evolved into a comrade in his quest for personal expression. As a result of this metamorphosis, he came to realise the actual power of art - the capacity to go beyond the bounds of what is imaginable and materialise the unthinkable.

Chapter 8: Painting the Impossible

As the sun rose, its warm rays filtered through the window, painting a beautiful art of light and shadow on the walls. Lesedi's eyes gently opened to the gentle touch of morning light. The room, with its warm and hopeful colours, embraced him as if it held secrets from the mystical world of dreams. The vibrant images of the magical paintbrush and the mysterious character, once so vivid, now faded into the realm of forgotten recollections. It felt as though the dream had dissolved into the atmosphere, leaving behind a hint of its enchantment lingering in the recesses of his thoughts.

Lesedi lay there for an instant, caught between the concreteness of his dream world and the immateriality of his awake existence. Although the magical paintbrush was now nothing more than a dream, it had left him with a legacy of inspiration that he carried with him, a legacy that spoke of opportunities for creative greatness and personal growth.

As he awoke from his sleep, the dream, fleeting like the mist of dawn, left a lasting impression. A sense of optimism and triumph resounded in his soul like the pleasant aftertaste of a dream. In the room, basking in the gentle morning sunlight, there was a serene sense of possibility. Even the most ephemeral dreams held the power to influence the reality that awaited.

As he embarked on a new day, the enigmatic visions delved further into the depths of his consciousness. In the depths of the night, the paintbrush danced with ethereal grace, while the mysterious Figure stood as a shadowy presence on the canvas of his imagination. With their departure, Lesedi was left to confront the rawness of life in the township, where obstacles and dreams intertwined.

In the early hours, the sun illuminated the township with an unforgiving glow, creating sharp contrasts that reflected the hardships ingrained in the streets.

As Lesedi entered the township, the echoes of his dream faded away, overshadowed by the harsh reality that surrounded him.

The streets, filled with stories of hardships and dreams, remained the same. The air was heavy with poverty, silently drifting through the narrow alleys and casting its shadow on the faces of those who walked them day after day. Lesedi walked through the day, becoming just another shadow in Sebokeng's cluttered tale.

Every stride along the well-known streets added a melancholic touch to the repetitive melody of Lesedi's daily life. The alleys, which were once brimming with the potential for inspiration, now appeared to be a conduit for the struggles that were deeply ingrained in Sebokeng's fabric. The routine, which used to be a soothing beat, had changed into a spooky tune that echoed the constant problems he was facing.

The routine felt like a never-ending rhythm, a constant reminder that echoed through every interaction, every glance shared in the bustling marketplace, and every colourful corner of Sebokeng. The rhythm of the day echoed the grand symphony of existence in Sebokeng—a melodic blend of challenges, resilience, and aspirations put on hold.

The routine became into a conductor of realities as he negotiated the tiny passageways, directing a play in which each scene underlined the stark differences that exist in reality. Similar to the way a dissonant chord disrupts a symphony, poverty cast a sombre note on the daily rhythm of life. The daily rituals that once held the allure of advancement now seemed more like a monotonous journey, a series of obstacles waiting to be overcome.

Amidst the cacophony of challenges, Lesedi held onto the dwindling melodies of his aspirations. The dreams of the mystical paintbrush and the enigmatic Figure felt far away, overshadowed by the noise of everyday existence, where the struggle for survival often took precedence over the pursuit of artistic aspirations.

Even though Lesedi was unable to recall his dream in the harsh light of day, it had left an indelible mark on his soul. He was enveloped by the feeling of triumph, as if it were a loyal companion that refused to let go. In the face of unforgiving streets and relentless challenges, a flame of resilience flickered within Lesedi. The dream's aftereffects were a gentle reminder that he could still unleash his inner artist and achieve amazing things no matter how difficult the day became. Lesedi discovered a method to align himself with the tune of his dreams, finding comfort in the notion that, just maybe, the melody could be transformed.

While Lesedi was struggling through the maze of unemployment, he embarked on a journey to find stability. As he proceeded through the world of job hunts, his movements had an air of calm resolve. The job market, reminiscent of an expansive and undiscovered terrain, offered its fair share of obstacles and possibilities. Careful attention was paid to the creation of resumes, with ambitions weaved into the language in an effort to convey the potential that he has inside himself.

As Lesedi searched carefully through the advertisements for employment, the experience turned into a surreal excursion, with each opening representing a possible future. Lesedi, filled with optimism and aspirations, navigated through the maze of interviews and job applications. The air was filled with the promise of endless opportunities, yet tinged with the apprehension that often accompanies the search for a job.

As he immersed himself in the process, the burden of responsibility weighed heavily on him. Every rejection seemed to blow with the force of a strong wind, ready to snuff out the fragile flame of hope. The process of looking for work turned into a dance of resiliency, consisting of a rhythmic succession of applications and interviews in which rejection and determination waltzed hand in hand.

Yet, even in the midst of challenges, Lesedi discovered a ray of optimism in the ordinary. The act of searching took on a profound significance, transforming into a pilgrimage that led him towards stability and served as a stepping stone towards his dreams. He embarked on a journey through unexplored realms, guided by the job listings that held the promise of new and exciting opportunities.

In the tapestry of his days, the pursuit of employment held a deeper significance.

It was a part of the bigger story of his dreams. Every application submitted, every interview attended, was a testament to his unwavering resolve. He pursued stability with unwavering determination, a testament to his unwavering strength. His journey was a captivating tale, eagerly awaiting the next chapter to unfold.

In the course of his hunt for a job, Lesedi expanded his search outside the bounds of the township, where he had previously located himself. He found unexpected riches within the everyday routine. Every day was an adventure, filled with a rich array of people and locations that opened his eyes to a world he had never imagined.

While he was walking through the busy streets of Jozi, he came across a collection of tales that he found to be a mosaic of challenges, successes, and desires that connected with the chords of his own aspirations. He encountered a multitude of faces, each with their own captivating stories, which he skilfully incorporated into the tapestry of his art. The city, with its symphony of sounds and vibrant array of colours, provided a rich canvas for his artistic expressions.

In the midst of this exploration, a spark of inspiration took root.

As Lesedi interacted with new people and immersed himself in a variety of settings, he developed a strong urge to communicate his own story to the rest of the world. Lesedi discovered an esteemed gallery space as if drawn by an invisible force, he found himself in front of the magnificence of a solo exhibition—hosted by a renowned South African artist - Tebogo Khalo. The walls were adorned with vibrant canvases, each telling a tale of its own, creating an atmosphere of awe and inspiration.

Lesedi found himself walking through the glass doors. The change from the busy street to the peaceful art area was almost dreamlike. The air inside was chilly and silent, with the faint aroma of fresh paint and polished wood.

The Gallery Attendant smiled kindly as Lesedi arrived, "Welcome. Please feel free to browse the show.

He nodded, almost controlling his enthusiasm. He walked through the exhibition, each step exposing masterpieces that appeared to throb with life. Tebogo Khalo's art was a symphony of colour and passion, with each piece presenting a tale that spoke strongly to him.

Lesesi said out loud and held his mouth, filled with delight and dread, "Tebogo Khalo? I have heard so much about him. His work is legendary." He whispers to himself, eyes wide with amazement, "This... this is incredible."

The exhibition was packed with visitors, all captivated by the vivid paintings and complex sculptures. However, Lesedi felt alone with the art, with each piece speaking straight to his soul. He stood in front of a particularly remarkable painting—a realistic depiction of Sebokeng life, full of detail and passion.

As he stood there, taking in the beauty and depth of Khalo's art, he felt a rush of inspiration. The misgivings that had troubled him appeared to vanish, replaced by a newfound feeling of purpose. Tebogo Khalo was able to push past the boundaries of the canvas, producing work that spoke to the essence of the human experience.

Tebogo approaches gently, seeing Lesedi intense focus, "I see you've found one of my favourites."

Surprised, he turned to face the artist, "Mr. Khalo! I...I am a huge fan of your work. It is an honour to meet you."

Tebogo grinned heartily and extended his hand. "The honour is mine. I am always glad to meet other art aficionados. What are your thoughts on the exhibition?

Lesedi shook his hand, his enthusiasm rising: "This... this is wonderful. The colours, the feelings... they are so vibrant. It is beyond words. Your painting is incredibly amazing. It talks to me like nothing else. How do you do it?"

Tebogo nodded appreciatively. "Thank you, but art emerges from the heart, from our most intimate experiences and feelings. It's about sharing our experiences and realities. Art has a way of bringing us together, doesn't it? It speaks to our common humanity."

Lesedi nodded excitedly. "Yes, it does. Your paintings feel so genuine and strong. They tell our stories."

"What about you? Are you an artist?" Tebogo studied Lesedi with interest.

Lesedi is apprehensive yet inspired. "I am. Or at least, I'm attempting to be. Sometimes it feels as if the weight of expectations is too much. But witnessing your art gives me hope."

"Every artist has these doubts, Lesedi. It is part of the trip. What important is that you keep producing and sharing your narrative. Art is a powerful agent of change, and we need voices like yours." Tebogo smiles encouragingly.

Called other visitors. Tebogo left Lesedi, and as he stood there, taking in the beauty and depth of Tebogo's art, Lesedi felt a rush of inspiration. The misgivings that had troubled him appeared to vanish, replaced by a newfound feeling of purpose.

For Lesedi, this unexpected meeting turned into a fortuitous occasion of creative connection. The strokes and hues, carefully selected by the featured artist, ignited a passion within him. The exhibition was more than just an art display; it was a vibrant celebration of stories, a harmonious blend of vivid hues and heartfelt emotions that deeply touched him.

With a deep sense of inspiration, Lesedi eagerly embraced the chance to fully engage in the artistic conversation. As he explored the gallery's intricate web of artistic expression, he saw an opportunity to expand the scope of his own storytelling. The radiant aspirations that had been ignited within the community resonated within the sophisticated halls of the gallery.

After this artistic journey, Lesedi experienced a newfound sense of purpose. Because of its art circles and galleries, the city ended up being more than simply a place where people might find employment; it also became a canvas for making connections and networking. In his mind, he saw his own solo exhibition not only as a reflection of personal success but also as a valuable addition to the diverse landscape of South African art.

As a result of this vision, Lesedi ventured into the world of well-known artists, curators, and authors, making use of the network that the city provided. He immersed himself in conversations, freely expressing his dreams, and crafted a captivating story that surpassed the limitations of the township.

As he embarked on the journey of preparing for his own exhibition, Lesedi carried the inspiration from a celebrated artist's exhibition. The dreams that burned brightly within him were kindled by his intense experiences, they soon became the brushstrokes that would grace the canvas of his solo show. In the city, pulsating with life, he found his inspiration—a place where the aspirations of the community intersected with the attention of the art world's most esteemed individuals.

The decision to pursue a solo exhibition wasn't just a practical move in response to the job market. It was a powerful affirmation of self-value and a joyous celebration of the stories that resonate within him. Every canvas, once a silent observer of the township's hardships, eagerly anticipated its chance to become a captivating narrator on a magnificent platform.

***

As the night enveloped him, Lesedi felt a renewed sense of energy as he made his way back to his studio. He possessed a fiery passion for the dreams that once wavered, now shining with unwavering intensity. Inspired by the artistic spirit, the brush gracefully danced across the canvas, creating a symphony of liberation. With each stroke, vibrant stories came to life, transcending the boundaries of the township.

The exhibition, in Lesedi's mind as he painted, was more than just a showcase of art; it was a representation of strength, optimism, and the capacity of aspirations to change lives. Not only would the walls of the gallery serve as a constant reminder of his individual journey, but they would also serve as a reflection of the collective spirit of a community that is working towards a better future.

Stories of perseverance and success were reflected in the paintings, which were now painted with the colours that he had envisioned for himself. Every brushstroke was a profound expression, a testament to the hidden narratives that dwelled within the soul of the community. Inspired by the enchanting power of creativity, the brush effortlessly weaved a captivating story that connected the challenges of everyday life with the dreams and ambitions of a wider audience.

Just as the night turned into day, Lesedi's studio became a haven of creative inspiration. In the gentle light of a single lamp, the canvases revealed a creative journey that had transcended uncertainty and embraced infinite potential.

In the intimate space of his studio, Lesedi's canvases came alive as silent observers and captivating narrators. Inspired by the enchanting world of art, every brushstroke became a graceful symphony of colours, breathing life into ethereal visions that carried tales of resilience, growth, and metamorphosis. The walls, as if captivated by the scene, embraced the unfolding story of the solo exhibition—a masterpiece coming to life within the artist's sacred haven.

Working through the night, the studio was filled with a vibrant energy of creativity. The brush moved with a rhythmic dance, capturing the anticipation that hung in the air. The solo show was already living, throbbing, and materialising by the time each stroke was completed, despite the fact that it was still a vision on the far horizon.

The canvases, once empty, now held the marks of Lesedi's intricate journey. Enchanting visions danced upon the canvas, weaving narratives that surpassed the boundaries of the physical realm. There was a symphony of colours that was waiting to be revealed to the world, and it was comprised of faces from the township, moments of silent resistance, and the echoes of dreams that were not voiced.

In the studio, a place where creativity thrived, was a haven of transformation. Within these four walls, Lesedi faced his doubts, questioned his perceptions, and gave life to the heart of his solo exhibition. The radiant dreams, akin to celestial protectors, observed in silence the profound metamorphosis taking place in their midst.

The solo exhibition was more than just an event—it was a culmination. It was the culmination of endless hours dedicated to perfecting his art, and transforming his radiant dreams into tangible stories, the essence of experiences gathered from the small town to the bustling metropolis. Every painting held a unique tale, coming together to create a rich tapestry of stories that echoed the desires of a community longing to have their voices heard.

The atmosphere in the studio was electric, filled with excitement and anticipation for the upcoming reveal. The radiant dreams appeared to glisten with a vitality of their own, yearning to break free from the boundaries of the artwork and sway beneath the illuminating gallery lights. Lesedi, in the midst of the vibrant world of brushes, pigments, and boundless inspiration, discovered a profound sense of peace as he witnessed his solo exhibition transform from a mere vision into a living embodiment, poised to make its mark in the rich tapestry of artistic expression.

The night before the exhibition was a whirlwind of emotions—nervous excitement intertwined with a sense of eager anticipation. Lesedi, immersed in his creations, stood in deep reflection. The radiant dreams, now pulsating with the vibrant energy of the city, appeared to shimmer with a renewed liveliness.

With the break of dawn, the day of the exhibition arrived, bringing forth a multitude of possibilities. Lesedi, filled with a blend of nervousness and satisfaction, cautiously carried his paintings to the gallery. The city, with its majestic skyscrapers and vibrant streets, served as the setting for this profound artistic revelation.

The gallery embraced Lesedi's work, where dreams came to life through vibrant colours and captivating forms. Stories of perseverance, optimism, and the transformational power of art were spoken by the paintings that were displayed in the museum with a dark lighting scheme. Every brushstroke in Lesedi's artwork told a story of resilience and triumph over adversity. Just like an enchanting tale waiting to be told, the gallery came alive as the radiant dreams adorned its immaculate walls.

The opening night arrived with the grandeur of a masterfully orchestrated symphony.

People from all walks of life, a diverse audience united by the allure of art, started to gather in the venue. Lesedi's radiant dreams, forged from the challenges of the township and the energy of the city, captivated every onlooker. As the audience meandered through the gallery, Lesedi's captivating story came to life right before their very eyes. The radiant dreams, once questioned and tested, now shone with a renewed energy. The colours swirled and twirled on the canvases, capturing the journey of an artist who defied all obstacles.

In the midst of the crowd, Lesedi stood, his eyes capturing the essence of the journey embedded in each stroke of the brush. Just like the way conversations buzzed around his work, the previously hushed voices of Sebokeng reverberated through the gallery. The ethereal dreams spoke a language that resonated with people from all walks of life, surpassing the limitations of location and situation. The solo exhibition took on a vibrant tapestry, intricately woven with Lesedi's challenges and victories. The narratives behind each artwork, revealed to those who were eager to delve into the artist's inner world, brought an extra dimension to the vivid exhibition. Once threatened by doubtful shadows, the glowing dreams now shone with the hope that art could go beyond the limits set by outside judgement.

The show, which was more than just a demonstration of creative skill, evolved into a demonstration of the resilient nature of dreams. Expressions of familiarity, affirming gestures, and hushed words of admiration merged into a shared understanding—an acknowledgement that art, when originating from the depths of one's being, has the power to surpass the boundaries of its medium.

The tenacity of Lesedi, which served as the unseen thread that held the show together, struck a chord with audience members who came into contact with his artwork. Through the transformation of the gallery into a place where hardships were changed into beauty and uncertainty was replaced by an assertion of creative identity, the gallery became a destination.

He discovered more than simply an audience as the show progressed; he also established a community whose members saw in the glowing visions common goals. A conversation that went beyond personal stories was born out of the once-daunting obstacles that brought the artist and the fan closer together.

A challenge to the established order was presented by the glowing dreams, which were now shown on the walls of the gallery. They encouraged spectators to challenge their preconceived conceptions of what art might be, pushing the limits of what was expected of them, and allowing them to envisage a world in which the cosmic and the ordinary coexisted.

On one side, a painting showcased a vibrant street in the township.

However, upon closer inspection, observers discovered that the street seamlessly merged into a celestial tapestry, adorned with constellations and nebulae. In a different realm, the members of the community underwent a profound metamorphosis, becoming celestial beings whose tales were eloquently conveyed through the graceful movements of the stars. Lesedi's profound understanding of the brush's immense potential was apparent in each artwork, encouraging viewers to contemplate the essence of existence.

As the night progressed, Lesedi discovered a newfound role as not only an artist but also a captivating storyteller. The ethereal dreams, now pulsating within the gallery's atmosphere, conveyed messages of optimism and potential. Those who were present at the show were able to feel the glowing storylines reverberate through their hearts because the city, which had before been a labyrinth of doubts, became a background for the stories.

In the same way that a phoenix emerges from the ashes of self-doubt, the solo show shed light not just on the walls of the gallery but also on the route that lies ahead. This path is now decorated with possibilities, challenges, and the never-ending dance of the cosmic brush.

The fusion of enchantment and creativity sparked enquiries into the moral consequences of defying established conventions. Some people believe that art should capture the tangible struggles of the community, serving as a reflection of the harsh realities they experience. Others, on the other hand, viewed Lesedi's work as a groundbreaking endeavour, shattering the limitations of traditional art and providing a glimpse into a realm where imagination had no limits.

The radiant dreams, now brought to life on the gallery walls, presented a formidable challenge to the established norms. They encouraged spectators to challenge their preconceived conceptions of what art might be, pushing the limits of what was expected of them, and allowing them to envisage a world in which the cosmic and the ordinary coexisted.

In the colourful world of the art community, a few sceptics couldn't help but raise their eyebrows at Lesedi's unique journey. Other artists, curators, and critics, who were used to more conventional stories of success, were amazed by his rapid rise but wondered if his newfound recognition would last.

As the night progressed, the ethical dilemma hung in the atmosphere, igniting discussions among the participants. Lesedi, immersed in this conversation, proudly stood next to his creations, silently urging the observers to embrace the transformative power of art and the limitless potential that exists outside of societal expectations. The exhibition sparked a conversation, a ripple in the pool of collective awareness, and encouraged community members to consider the power of creativity in liberating the human spirit, beyond just showcasing creative genius.

The scepticism that Lesedi encountered did not prevent him from seeing it as a chance to further hone his skill. His tenacity was fuelled by the rumours of uncertainty, and he channelled this energy into the creation of art that not only enthralled the audience but also silenced those who were sceptical.

In tandem with the progression of his luminous visions, the ways in which his artwork was seen by the art world also continued to develop. Lesedi wholeheartedly embraced the challenge of demonstrating that his achievements were not mere fleeting moments, but rather a testament to the profound impact of resilience and choosing unconventional paths.

Lesedi's work took centre stage during a pivotal art event, marking a turning point in his career. The doubters, who had previously shown doubt, now found themselves captivated by the radiant stories he crafted. The paintings conveyed a powerful narrative, capturing the essence of a visionary who fearlessly challenged conventional norms.

The whispers of the attendees filled the gallery, a chorus of voices engaged in passionate discussions about Lesedi's artistic rebellion. Many were enchanted by the allure of escaping the limitations of traditional art, embracing the enchanting realism that Lesedi's brush had revealed. They viewed it as a tribute to the remarkable possibilities concealed within the mundane.

Others, on the other hand, held onto what they knew. Some people wondered if the combination of enchantment and real-life situations lessened the genuineness of the challenges portrayed in the artwork. It was a profound ethical quandary that reverberated in the thoughts of those in attendance, the conflict between established customs and groundbreaking ideas, between the security of familiarity and the captivating appeal of the unfamiliar.

Lesedi, immersed in his creations, experienced the burden of these opposing viewpoints. His work, a reflection of his personal journey, had unintentionally sparked a deeper contemplation within society. The glowing visions, which were once a source of personal inspiration, have now spurred a communal discussion on the role that art plays in moulding views and defying conventions.

The gallery, illuminated by the gentle radiance of the displayed artworks, transformed into a vibrant arena of thoughts and perspectives. Deep philosophical questions emerged, pondering the moral obligations that artists have towards their communities. Lesedi's artistic talent transcended the boundaries of the canvas, revealing a world where the extraordinary seamlessly intertwined with the ordinary.

As the night progressed, the exhibition began to take on a

captivating essence. The radiant dreams appeared to throb with a vitality that surpassed the confines of the tangible realm. It was a powerful demonstration of how art has the ability to transform, reminding us that creativity can reshape our views and question societal norms.

Positive reviews poured in, not only from art enthusiasts but also from those who had initially questioned Lesedi's unorthodox path. Not only did the glowing visions become a sign of creative skill, but they also became a strong tale of triumphing over scepticism and prospering in spite of hardship.

Lesedi's success had a profound impact on other artists, encouraging them to embrace their own individual journeys. The former sceptics, now transformed into admirers, recognised the genuine and profound nature of Lesedi's work. They came to understand that thinking outside the box could result in remarkable achievements in the world of creativity.

As Lesedi's glowing ideas went beyond question, the story went from being sceptical to being admiring. Renowned in the art community, he is now hailed as a visionary who defies conventions and revolutionises the concept of artistic achievement.

Inspired by the wisdom of great minds, his sceptics faded into mere whispers, overshadowed by the symphony of his remarkable achievements. Inspired by the brilliance of visionary artists, their radiant dreams have captivated a wider audience, casting a luminous glow on both gallery walls and the creative journeys of those who dare to explore the uncharted realms of unconventional artistic expression.

In the aftermath of the solo show, Lesedi discovered that the profound force of his work was the source of his peace, rather than the quick notoriety or financial success he had been seeking. Following their departure from the limits of the museum, the glowing dreams set off on a voyage of their own. A lasting presence in the hearts and minds of the community, they were ingrained in the history of people who had experienced the exhibition and formed a part of the collective memory of those individuals.

The brilliance of creative expression had pushed the shadows of uncertainty, tenacious as they were, to the margins. Lesedi's journey, filled with obstacles and difficulties, became a powerful example of the timeless impact of storytelling through art. Inspired by the spirit of great writers, the ethereal dreams became woven into the fabric of the community, painting a vivid picture of strength and the limitless potential that arises when we face our darkest fears with the boldness of artistic bravery.

Despite the fact that the artist was still facing financial difficulties and demands from the outside world, the luminous visions served as a reminder that the genuine influence of art frequently extends beyond the immediate challenges that an artist must overcome. Lesedi, in his ongoing artistic pursuits, emerged as a storyteller who not only expressed himself but also connected with the community, sharing in the joys and challenges of his creative journey.

With the gallery doors shutting behind him, Lesedi bore the burden of unfulfilled expectations and the confidence that he had crafted a story that went beyond the fleeting nature of achievement. The radiant dreams, despite being dimmed by external obstacles, still shimmered in the shared awareness of those who had witnessed the exhibition.

Chapter 9: The Colors of Destiny

I n the quiet aftermath of the exhibition, the gallery stood as a haven of metamorphosis.

The ethereal dreams on the canvases appeared to possess a vitality of their own, whispered stories that exceeded the mere brushstrokes of paint. Lesedi, with his unique artistic vision, became a central figure in a conversation that expanded far beyond what was possible.

As the morning light filtered into the gallery, Lesedi strolled through the lingering whispers of conversations from the previous night. Art critics pondered the delicate balance between the mystical and the tangible, seeking to unravel the ethereal quality imbued in each stroke of the brush. Ethicists engaged in a lively discussion regarding the moral obligations of artists whose works transcend the boundaries of the canvas and have an extensive effect on the shared consciousness of a community.

Outside the gallery, the sebokeng buzzed with a blend of wonder and doubt.

Lesedi's introduction of magical realism challenged not only artistic norms but also societal expectations, evoking a sense of wonder and pushing boundaries. The moral dilemma was unmistakable, lingering in the atmosphere as if it were a query in need of resolution.

The radiant dreams on the canvases captivated the attention of inquisitive individuals and ignited discussions that reverberated throughout the community. In the midst of these discussions, Lesedi felt the immense responsibility he carried, not only towards his craft, but also towards the community that had fostered his artistic spirit.

Even in the midst of the discussions and moral contemplation, there was an unmistakable sense of shift. The line between imagination and reality appeared to blur, and the previously unknown regions of artistic expression now beckoned the community to imagine a future painted with the colours of possibility.

Shortly following the result of the exhibition, Lesedi found himself at a pivotal moment, torn between the familiar and the unknown. The luminescent dreams, which everyone in Sebokeng now remembers, made them think about how limited their own imaginations really were. The magic in his art started a conversation that went beyond the gallery walls and into the hearts and minds of those who were brave enough to dream with him.

Local media outlets, drawn by the buzz surrounding the debate, flocked to the gallery for interviews. Lesedi, exuding the essence of an unexpected leader, found himself at the forefront of a movement he hadn't initially set out to guide.

News of Lesedi's groundbreaking exhibition caused a stir in the art world, with both praise and criticism. Critics were intrigued by the blending of enchantment and reality, challenging the limits of artistic creativity. Supporters, however, viewed Lesedi as a visionary who dared to question the established norms and explore the limitless possibilities of art.

In the midst of the external debates, Lesedi found himself grappling with an internal conflict. He was deeply troubled by the moral dilemma that his art unintentionally brought about. Was he an artist who challenged the norms and pushed boundaries, or was he someone who caused tension within his community? The question reverberated in his thoughts, a steadfast companion as he sought solace in his studio.

At first, people in the neighbourhood had different opinions about Lesedi's art. But over time, more and more people came to agree that creation doesn't have to follow strict rules. As a result of the luminous dreams, people began talking about the latent potential in their town. Lesedi's art, which worked to bring about change, was no longer just displayed in a gallery. It had seeped into people's minds and sparked a desire for change.

In spite of all the obstacles and unknowns, Lesedi was a trailblazer for a new movement in creative inquiry. The magical realism that permeated his works became an emblem of optimism, a reminder that pushing limits may pave the way for social progress. As he continued to paint, Lesedi wrestled with the contradiction of embracing tradition while also pushing boundaries, preserving his community's stories while also envisioning its untapped potential.

In perfect synchrony, the radiant dreams embraced the challenges of Sebokeng, defying any doubts about their existence in the real world. Not only did Lesedi's artwork become a mirror that reflected the complexities of his own journey, but it also reflected the intricate fabric of a community that was continuously changing. The cosmic brush, sensitive to his innermost feelings and ideas, created a story that went beyond the tangible and into the fantastic.

Lesedi's artistic journey pushed the boundaries of reality, taking Sebokeng on an extraordinary evolution. In his paintings, a world of wonder and enchantment seamlessly merged with the challenges and realities of everyday existence.

Sebokeng was adorned with vivid murals that brought life to once-neglected walls, turning them into symbols of resistance and hope. Every brushstroke of the universe's canvas reverberated with tales of victory and narratives of a community determined to transcend its obstacles.

Nevertheless, the incorporation of magic into his art sparked profound discussions. Many admired Lesedi for his unique perspective and the way his work breathed life into the community. Others, though, raised concerns about the implications of blurring the boundaries between what is real and what is imagined. There were lingering ethical concerns, driven by the uncertainty of the potential outcomes of this artistic exploration.

Lesedi, immersed in the midst of these discussions, discovered comfort in the very streets he depicted on canvas. As he strolled through the township, he couldn't help but notice the profound effect his work had on the faces of those who experienced it. Having gone beyond the sphere of art, the luminous visions became an integral part of the community's story, igniting discussions and motivating a shared rethinking of possibilities.

Lesedi's artistic journey was marked by a moral dilemma that consistently found its way into his work. His paintings were more than just a record of his thoughts; they were pleas for viewers to question where truth and fantasy intersect, as well as the limits of tradition and creativity. Every artwork posed a thought-provoking question, urging the observer to question their own assumptions and defy the conventional standards that shaped their perception of art.

But even as Lesedi continued to explore his creative side, he couldn't escape the sense that he was standing on the edge of something. Thanks to the mystical properties it possessed, the cosmic brush had evolved into a medium that allowed for both individual and collective self-reflection. While the ethical conundrums that he incorporated into his artwork served as threads that connected him to the pulse of the community, each stroke carried the weight of the aspirations of the community as a whole.

The art world, filled with anticipation and caution, eagerly awaited Lesedi's upcoming revelation. In the past, the glowing dreams were restricted to the canvas; however, today they were dancing in the thoughts of people who watched them. Everyone in the village looked at its own potential through the lens of his magical realism work. It made them question and rethink the limits that held their dreams back.

As Lesedi struggled to make sense of the complexity of his work, he discovered that he was at the crossroads of change and tradition. In his grasp, the cosmic brush hummed with a potent blend of enchantment and truth, poised to weave the next vibrant tapestry of his artistic journey. This chapter would not only reshape his personal narrative but also question the very essence of the community he held dear.

After Lesedi's groundbreaking art sparked debates, Sebokeng

stood on the brink of change. Lesedi, admired by many for his visionary art, faced the challenges of societal expectations. In seeking an artist who could guide them through uncharted territories of transformation, the township wholeheartedly embraced his magical realism.

The local council, reminiscent of the rich tapestry of the community, gathered to deliberate on the influence of Lesedi's art. They couldn't help but wonder if the cosmic brush was a symbol of progress or a potential threat to the status quo, as scepticism and curiosity intertwined.

The local media gave voice to the ethical dilemmas surrounding his work. Journalists engaged in a lively discussion about the delicate balance between artistic expression and societal responsibility, pondering whether Lesedi's art showcased innovation or ventured into the realm of the unknown.

As the community engaged in a thought-provoking conversation inspired by his art, Lesedi wrestled with the profound sense of duty. In the realm of artistic expression, the brush that once brought forth personal enlightenment has now transformed into a powerful emblem of shared dreams and ambitions. His paintings took on a new dimension, becoming reflections of the hopes, challenges, and aspirations of an entire community.

Lesedi's art unexpectedly found allies amidst these debates. Local educators recognised the potential of his work to ignite creativity in the younger generation. They wanted art classes that transcended traditional limits, encouraging students to delve into the enchantment of their own creative minds.

Community leaders, who were initially doubtful, started to recognise the economic possibilities of Lesedi's art. The captivating dreams had caught the eye of people from outside the township, enticing tourists and art enthusiasts. Lesedi's murals exude a captivating aura, leading visitors on a profound artistic odyssey.

However, obstacles continued to arise. There were those in the community who clung tightly to their traditions, unwilling to embrace the winds of change. Lesedi, with a deep understanding of the importance of finding harmony, initiated discussions with individuals who were concerned about the evolving environment of their residence.

Lesedi, through collaborative murals and community projects, aimed to blend the essence of tradition with the vibrant fabric of transformation. It was not his intention to forget the past; rather, he wanted to reinvent it, to pay homage to the foundations while enabling the branches to fly towards the skies.

Lesedi learnt the real strength of art as he moved through this complex dance: its capacity to unite people, spark dialogue, and create a common story for a whole culture. The moral dilemmas, which were once cast as dark clouds, have now become chances for us to reflect together.

In the heart of Sebokeng, where history whispered tales of hardship and the future called out with the potential for growth, Lesedi's art served as a connection between the old ways and the new possibilities. These glowing dreams, which were only seen on painting before, were now pulsing through the town like the heartbeat of its people.

As the sun gracefully descended beneath the horizon, casting enchanting shadows on the well-known streets, Lesedi's murals burst into vibrant life. A bright force was now vibrating through the walls, which had been quiet witnesses to the passage of time in the past. The radiant dreams had intertwined with the essence of Sebokeng, creating a vibrant story of strength and potential.

Every brushstroke on the canvas revealed a profound conversation between the past and the present. Scenes of hope and transformation emerged on walls that had weathered decades of hardship, reminiscent of the works of a renowned author. Wise elders observed captivating murals that depicted a future where past hardships were transformed into opportunities for a better future.

Under the soft glow of the streetlamps, a group of children huddled together, captivated by the enchanting murals that adorned the walls. They were able to kindle their imaginations and light the fires of aspiration with the glowing visions that were now a part of their nightly stories. The young ones perceived Lesedi's art as more than just paintings; they saw it as gateways to realms where their aspirations could manifest.

Lesedi, like an artist with a cosmic brush in hand, felt the immense weight of responsibility. The moral dilemmas entwined within his art were now reflected in the gaze of those who witnessed it. Because of his work, the customary limitations of creative expression had been surpassed, and it had become a catalyst for societal contemplation.

The elders, at first hesitant, became engaged in discussions ignited by the murals. They contemplated the contrast between tradition and innovation, acknowledging that Lesedi's art seamlessly combined the old and the new without posing a threat to their heritage. Rather than seeing the glowing visions as a break from their story, Sebokeng came to see them as an extension of it.

While Lesedi was making his way through the murky waters of tradition and change, he came to understand that creating art was about more than just him. The ethereal dreams, gracefully moving across the walls, whispered the hopes and aspirations of the community. Every brushstroke became a powerful symbol of collective dreams, and each mural served as a powerful testament to the boundless potential of art.

Attuned to the world around him, Lesedi felt the rhythm of Sebokeng, a hidden bond that linked his art to the shared pulse of his community. It wasn't just painted strokes that made the dreams glow; they were echoes of shared hopes, an artistic conversation with the hopes that echoed through the busy streets and tight alleys.

The murals, created through a divine artistic process, were not merely Lesedi's visions, but rather reflections of the collective spirit. As he painted, he sensed the essence of his neighbours, the untold tales of hardship and strength entwined within every stroke. The cosmic brush, charged with the spirit of community aspirations, connected his personal story to Sebokeng's collective history.

Lesedi's art resonated with the essence of tradition, paying homage to the rich stories woven into the tapestry of Sebokeng's history. However, it was a courageous declaration of change, encouraging the community to envision a new story for itself. The murals dared to defy convention, beckoning observers to ponder the boundaries they had become accustomed to and envision a world adorned with the colours of endless potential.

The ethical discussions that revolved around Lesedi's work were essentially debates about the future of Sebokeng. Every brushstroke raised a profound question for the community. It challenged them to explore the limits of convention and contemplate the sacrifices they were willing to make in order to capture the enchantment infused within the paintings.

However, amidst these discussions, there was an undeniable allure in the radiant aspirations. They were a celebration of resiliency, a demonstration of the potential of the human spirit to bring forth artistic expression in the face of hardship. Previously silent witnesses to adversity, the walls suddenly resounded with the harmonic buzz of those who had the potential to succeed.

As Lesedi painted, he experienced a profound sense of responsibility. His work went beyond mere exhibition; it served as a catalyst for the community to perceive itself in a new light. Through the merging of tradition and transformation, the cosmic brush hinted of a future where Sebokeng's tale will be moulded not just by its past but also by the brilliant aspirations of its inhabitants.

Immersed in the serene moments of creation, Lesedi came to a profound realisation - his artistic journey was deeply intertwined with the essence of the community. Not only were the glowing aspirations, which emerged from the delicate balance between tradition and change, displayed on the walls; they were imprinted on the collective mind as well, calling upon the township to rise above the gloom of its history and embrace a dynamic, rethought future.

Lesedi served as the guardian of the communal dreams that were shown in this luminous tapestry, which was a place where reality and magic interacted with one another. It was a story that cherished the township's past, welcomed its present, and dared to dream of a future in which the frontiers of what was conceivable went far beyond the horizon. The cosmic brush, which had become a symbol of unification, continued to paint the changing narrative of the township.

Once contained to the canvas, the luminous visions now soared across the township's winding alleyways and busy streets like ethereal butterflies. And Lesedi's brushstrokes were like notes in a beautiful song. His art resonated not only in the minds of those who saw it but also in the hearts of everyone in the community.

People of various backgrounds, whether they were experienced art enthusiasts or casual observers, were captivated by the vibrant tapestry that adorned the walls. It wasn't merely about the strokes and colours; it was also about the encompassed stories woven within the ethereal dreams, the tales of adversity, victory, and the interconnectedness of humanity.

Life is a beautiful symphony of emotions.

The ripple effect began gently, reminiscent of a gentle breeze carrying the scent of blooming inspiration. People in Sebokeng were filled with awe and wonder when they came across the murals. People from all walks of life were captivated by Lesedi's paintings, creating a sense of unity and connection. It transformed into a collective adventure, a voyage together through the spectrum of feelings depicted on the walls.

People engaged in conversations about the art, discovering common threads through the visual stories. As a means of communication, the luminous dreams served to unite individuals and break down barriers. It was no longer solely about the artwork; it had become about the profound sense of unity it evoked.

As news travelled, the impact extended far beyond the township.

Visitors flocked from nearby towns, captivated by the enchantment of this creative sanctuary. The radiant dreams became an irresistible allure, drawing in those in search of inspiration and an escape from the ordinary. Lesedi's art had become a place that people sought out, a powerful example of how creativity can change lives.

Amidst the beautiful symphony of emotions, a feeling of

harmony arose.

Everyone felt like they belonged in Sebokeng, which had transformed from a collection of individual lives into a shared canvas. The murals turned everyday places into stages for the unusual, providing a background for community events, meetings, and celebrations.

Dreams that shimmered with light persisted in their enchanting web.

The influence that Lesedi's work had on people who met it went beyond the immediate; it had a lasting mark on their hearts and minds. The symphony continued to play, a melody that grew and embraced the beauty of collective narratives and the harmony found in the strokes of an imaginative painter.

In the middle of the township, where the ancient cobblestone streets were woven with unknown tales, Lesedi wove a colourful tapestry of glowing aspirations into the scenery. As the sun sank beneath the horizon, enveloping the painted walls in a gentle, golden light, the township came alive with a renewed appreciation for art.

Locals, who have embraced the routine of daily life, now find themselves captivated by the streets, becoming intrigued explorers in their own community. The murals were more than just paintings; they served as gateways to the collective history, challenges, and victories of the people. Inspired by the essence of life, Lesedi's brushstrokes breathed life into a gallery that captured the soul of the township.

Visitors from nearby regions gathered to witness the extraordinary event, transforming the township into a vibrant centre of artistic pilgrimage. As they walked through the narrow alleys, the radiant dreams shared stories that went beyond cultural limits. Lesedi's paintings have a profound ability to connect with people on a deep, emotional level, transcending language barriers.

The murals were alive, capturing the ever-changing story of the community.

A lively mural in the marketplace captured the energy and liveliness of everyday life, with the faces of the crowd reflecting the expressions of the onlookers. A mural on a worn-out wall depicted the indomitable spirit of the people, exemplified by a solitary tree proudly defying the challenges it faced.

It wasn't just a straight line through the township when it turned into a living gallery; the streets were full of stories just ready to be discovered. The walls beckoned with their tales, urging us to immerse ourselves in their stories. Conversations ignited among people passing by, as they exchanged their own interpretations of the radiant dreams. Just like the way art brings people together, the murals served as gathering spots for individuals who quickly formed connections and friendships.

Sebokeng's transformation went beyond what met the eye; it represented a profound change in culture. Art became a language that brought people together, fostering a sense of unity and shared identity. Local businesses enthusiastically embraced the creative wave, decorating their shopfronts with vibrant murals that celebrated the spirit of the community. The rhythm of artistic appreciation resonated with every footstep, a melodic flow that surpassed the ordinary.

Once contained to the canvas, Lesedi's paintings have now seeped into Sebokeng's collective mind. The murals were more than mere reflections; they beckoned for collective engagement, celebration, and dreaming. The streets, vibrant and filled with stories, served as a powerful reminder of how art can shape and define a community's identity.

In the midst of the township's changing scenery, Lesedi's art emerged as a captivating force that caught the attention of the broader art community. Art galleries, once considered exclusive and distant, now eagerly sought the ethereal beauty that radiated from his paintings. Lesedi's doorstep was graced by the long-awaited arrival of recognition.

Art enthusiasts and critics were captivated by the intricate tapestry he created, a mesmerising blend of the ethereal and the concrete. Inspired by the enchanting strokes of a master artist, these captivating brushstrokes have captivated the hearts of art enthusiasts worldwide.

Galleries were excited to display the profound impact of Lesedi's art and eagerly sent out invitations for exhibitions. The radiant aspirations were to venture beyond the local community, embracing a worldwide audience. Lesedi, a once reserved dreamer in the alleys, now found himself at a pivotal moment of recognition, where the art world not only appreciated his talent but also recognised the profound narratives conveyed through his paintings.

As Lesedi's work received praise from reviews and articles, he found himself venturing into a realm he had only ever glimpsed in his dreams. The admiration extended beyond his technical skills to the profound emotional impact of his art—a connection between the extraordinary and the profoundly human.

When Lesedi was in the thick of openings for galleries and interviews, he managed to keep his feet on the ground by relying on the stories of the township that served as the source of his inspiration. Acknowledgement wasn't only about his own success; it was a chance to provide a stronger voice to those who had supported him through thick and thin.

The radiant aspirations, reminiscent of the works of a

renowned author, were now poised to embark on a worldwide journey. Lesedi, the artist, stood on the edge of a new chapter, where his creations would go beyond physical boundaries and challenge the norms of traditional art. His talent was not only recognised, but also acknowledged as a universal language that resonated with the human spirit across continents.

In the serene halls of art galleries, Lesedi's radiant dreams discovered a fresh abode.

The walls, reminiscent of the human experience, resonated with the indomitable spirit that transcends beyond. He was celebrated not just for his artistic talent, but for the profound impact his brushstrokes had on the world.

As visitors wandered through the sacred corridors, they encountered more than just paintings. Instead, they were immersed in narratives that intertwined tales of hardship, aspirations, and the unyielding resilience of the human soul. Lesedi's art has transcended boundaries, captivating audiences worldwide. The radiant aspirations, once softly murmured in the streets, now resounded boldly in the realm of cosmic unity.

Galleries, usually associated with the upper class, welcomed the radiant aspirations with enthusiasm. Many critics were captivated by the enchanting blend of imagination and reality found in Lesedi's paintings, which pushed the boundaries of traditional art. Every canvas transformed into a gateway, beckoning viewers into a realm where the mundane intertwined with the magical.

The recognition and praise were not only for Lesedi, but also for the township.

It was a celebration of the stories that had been longing to be heard for so long. Emblems of a community's strength were conveyed by the luminous aspirations, which were now performed on a worldwide platform.

However, in the midst of all the glitz and excitement of exhibitions and the art world, Lesedi stayed grounded. He viewed recognition not as a pedestal, but rather as a duty - a duty to keep sharing stories and serving as a channel for the voices that required amplification.

Inspired by the enchanting power of storytelling, the artist's work effortlessly crossed geographical boundaries, weaving together vivid dreams that resonated with people around the world. Lesedi, Sebokeng artist, captured the essence of the human experience through his captivating stories, serving as a conduit for shared struggles and aspirations. Rather than letting him forget his humble beginnings, the fame served as a means to transport his luminous aspirations to regions where optimism was both a common language and an invaluable commodity.

In the midst of this recognition, Lesedi stayed humble, finding satisfaction not in the praise of the art world, but in the appreciation of those who viewed his paintings as something beyond mere art. To them, his works were mirrors of their own narratives. An entire new generation of creative thinkers and dreamers was inspired as a result of the ripple effect that spread across the community.

In the maze of narrow streets, Lesedi's presence transcended that of an artist, it was a vibrant tale that came to life. There was a time when Sebokeng was covered in the cloak of battle, but now it was covered in the fabric of bright hopes. Every step Lesedi took resonated with a profound sense of gratitude and joy, as if the atmosphere itself whispered words of appreciation.

Once contained in paintings, the luminous visions are now part of a shared story and the collective mind of the community. Walking through the familiar alleys, Lesedi felt a strong sense of unity, a collective pride that reverberated in the air. Sebokeng had undergone a profound transformation, not only in its outward appearance, but also in its essence.

The residents, who were once acquaintances, now saw Lesedi as a source of inspiration. His path from uncertainty to success reflected their shared determination. Once mute spectators to difficulties, the lanes now buzzed with stories of success from those who had overcome them.

Children playing in the streets would stop and gaze at Lesedi, their eyes filled with wonder and inspiration as they admired his captivating brushstrokes. Elders nodded in agreement, recognising in him a living example of how creativity can overcome challenges. Lesedi had transcended the realm of mere artistry, embodying the essence of a profound allegory, a testament to the profound potential hidden within the ethereal realm of vivid aspirations.

He had engraved a tale into the very fabric of Sebokeng, a story that transcended the confines of language, with every brush-stroke and mural he had created. As a result of the luminous aspirations seeping into the base, a sense of communal pride emerged that was more illuminating than any piece of art.

As Lesedi strolled through the township, he bore not only the burden of recognition but also the duty of safeguarding dreams. Walking through the alleys, Lesedi witnessed the transformation of the community. The dreams had taken on a life of their own, infusing the surroundings with a radiant energy. The stories of hope and resilience now bound the people together, creating a vibrant tapestry of shared experiences.

As Lesedi navigated the streets, an undeniable aura of determination emanated from him. The luminous fantasies that he painted were not merely strokes on a canvas; rather, they were brushstrokes of hope, clear reminders that creativity might emerge as a transformational force to emerge from the furnace of suffering.

Lesedi's art had a profound impact that extended well beyond the confined streets of Sebokeng. There was a certain energy that coursed through the veins of all those who experienced the radiant dreams. It seemed as if the vivid colours were whispering tales of resiliency and the limitless possibilities that might be unleashed when imagination danced with the darkness.

The impact reached people of all ages and backgrounds. Lesedi was a symbol of hope for the children who looked at his work with awe. In his luminescent brushstrokes, elders found a reflection of a shared history and a glimpse of a brighter future, nodding their approval.

Lesedi had unknowingly assumed the role of a guardian of hope, a living embodiment of the notion that art, when created with genuine sincerity, has the power to go beyond mere paint on a canvas and deeply resonate with a community's spirit. The radiant dreams, ingrained in the shared awareness, were not mere still pictures; they were captivating narratives that unfurled with every lingering glance.

People from all walks of life, who have experienced Lesedi's work, discovered a mutual understanding and admiration for the profound impact of creativity. The radiant dreams had become a bridge, linking hearts across diverse backgrounds. It felt as though Lesedi's brush had captured a language that resonated deeply with the human spirit.

In the hushed corners of the township and beyond, discussions buzzed about the radiant aspirations. They were not only admired, but also the subject of discussion, interpretation, and embrace. Lesedi's purpose, evident in every brushstroke, ignited a conversation about the power of art to surpass limitations and cultivate harmony.

In the depths of Lesedi's artistic process, his brush transformed into a powerful instrument of transformation. With each stroke, he wove a magnificent tapestry of hope that extended far beyond the boundaries of his own existence. Everyone who saw the glowing ideas could speak the same language. They showed how imagination can change things and leave an indelible mark on people's hearts and minds.

In the tranquil moments of the evening, as the final beams of sunlight cast a beautiful palette of colours across the sky, Lesedi found himself in the midst of streets adorned with his radiant aspirations. He felt an overwhelming sense of gratitude, as if the very air around him was filled with whispers of appreciation.

The murals, illuminated by the fading sunlight, appeared to possess a vitality that surpassed the boundaries of paint and fabric. They exuded a certain magic, these individuals, their lives serving as living testaments to the profound impact of artistic expression. Inspiration flowed through the hearts of many as each stroke of his brush painted scenes that wove a tapestry of beauty.

The influence of the ripple, which had begun as a mere whisper of potential, had now developed into a torrent of inspiration. It wandered through the town, impacting the lives of those who stopped to witness the radiant aspirations. Lesedi's art had transcended its physical form, weaving a tapestry of human connection and shared stories that resonated deeply with those who experienced it.

Immersed in a world of radiant dreams, Lesedi transcended his role as an artist and transformed into a captivating storyteller, whose narratives resonated deeply within the souls of passersby. He felt immense gratitude, not only for the recognition he received, but also for the profound impact his art had on awakening the collective consciousness.

People walked by, their eyes shining with the spark of inspiration ignited by the murals. Conversations thrived, brimming with interpretations, emotions, and a collective sense of accomplishment. The streets, which had been mute witnesses to challenges in the past, now rang with the pulse of a community that was brought together by luminous hopes.

During that magical moment, Lesedi experienced a deep realisation of the immense power of art. The community was led through the darkness of uncertainty by his murals, which were more than just decorative elements; they were guiding lights of belief. As the sun dipped below the horizon, the river of inspiration continued its course, taking with it the spirit of Lesedi's creative voyage.

In the twilight hours, the ethereal dreams persisted, enveloping the town in an enchanting ambiance. Lesedi's appreciation hung in the air, a quiet recognition of the profound impact of art in transcending barriers, enlightening spirits, and, above all, fostering a collective aspiration to envision a shared future.

Chapter 10: The Legacy of Colors

After Lesedi's artistic journey, Sebokeng changed in ways that went beyond the glowing dreams that were painted on the walls. Lesedi, a talented artist who faced many challenges and uncertainties, has now become a source of inspiration for the community, leaving a lasting impact on their artistic journey.

There were many shades of change in Sebokeng as the new year began. Once walking through the dark alleys of doubt, Lesedi became a source of inspiration, creating a story that went beyond the painting and became a part of the community's very structure.

His work, reminiscent of the enchantment of a magician, gracefully meandered through the bustling streets, leaving an indelible mark on the souls of the community and igniting a sense of wonder within. The murals, inspired by the enchanting visions, were more than just paintings; they were vibrant tales engraved on the walls, tales that softly spoke of strength and whispered of optimism.

As the citizens of the town strolled down those streets, they were not just crossing concrete and brick; rather, they were wandering through an open gallery of imaginative possibilities. A rhythmic story of triumph over hardship was told with each stroke of Lesedi's brush, which reflected the heartbeat of the community they represent.

The change was unmistakable. Once awash in the greyscale of conflict, the township has now blossomed into a rainbow of hues. Lesedi's radiant dreams, having shattered the shackles of uncertainty, gracefully twirled upon the walls, narrating stories of a transformative voyage from darkness to vividness.

The group, which had been divided by difficulties in the past, discovered togetherness through the sharing of stories of glowing dreams. Lesedi's art was a profound exchange that effortlessly connected the artist with the community, surpassing language and obstacles.

Lesedi, who had experienced the hardships of being an artist, had become a beacon of creative expression. His murals, which were so colourful and full of life, helped the township navigate through storms of uncertainty and shed light on a route that led to limitless creativity. The winding lanes, which had been plagued by unpredictability in the past, had become corridors of opportunity.

The legacy of Lesedi's creative journey was not limited to the walls of art galleries or art studios; rather, it was embodied in the grins of youngsters who saw their ambitions mirrored in the murals, in the conversations that were generated by the paintings, and in the revitalised feeling of pride that reverberated throughout the streets.

And thus, Sebokeng's metamorphosis was not merely a result of paint on walls—it stood as a testament to the profound impact of art. Lesedi's radiant dreams had transformed into a mirror, capturing not only his artistic success but also the shared triumph of a community that had embraced the power of vibrant and brilliant imagination.

Reflecting on his growth, Lesedi realised that the true legacy lay not in the murals themselves, but in the profound impact they had on the hearts of Sebokeng residents. His work had evolved into a tale of strength, a narrative conveyed not only through vibrant hues but through the indomitable spirit of a community triumphing over adversity.

In the serene pauses amidst Lesedi's artistic strokes, a profound metamorphosis unfolded within the realm of family. The previously tumultuous dynamics, filled with doubt and miscommunication, seemed to fade away in the radiant light of Lesedi's triumph.

The ethereal dreams that graced the township's walls also cast their enchantment within the confines of Lesedi's humble abode. In the eyes of the family, the magical paintbrush changed from an enigmatic omen to a source of great pride, representing their collective accomplishments.

Lesedi's artistic journey had created a beautiful tapestry, weaving threads of understanding and unity into the fabric of familial relationships. His mother now stood with a radiant smile, her eyes shining with the pride she felt for her son. The brother, who was once perplexed by the enigmatic paintbrush, now viewed it as a gateway to a world where artistic expression had the power to profoundly change lives.

The radiant dreams had not only beautified the town, but had also created a collective tapestry of dreams within the family. Lesedi's success became a bridge, connecting them and bridging the gaps of doubt and misunderstanding that had once kept them apart. The walls of doubt fell away, revealing a beautiful painting of love and encouragement from my loved ones.

With each new installation, Lesedi's art strengthened the community's already-fragile relationships by changing its outward appearance. His family experienced the enchanting dreams that filled their home and touched their hearts.

In the midst of shared triumph, Lesedi's mother and brother provided steadfast support, standing by his side as he continued to create the unimaginable, not only on canvases but in the very fabric of their intertwined lives.

His artistic journey had a profound impact that reached far beyond his family and Sebokeng. It had a profound impact on the wider art community, leaving a lasting impression on the world of creative expression. The radiant dreams had transcended mere canvases; they embodied a spirit of strength, optimism, and the profound ability of art to bring about change.

His success resonated not just in the vivid brushstrokes on his canvases, but also in the hearts of aspiring artists who found inspiration in his ability to unlock the boundless potential of creativity. He had transcended the uncertain paths he once treaded and now served as a wellspring of inspiration for a new wave of individuals.

The community used to be held back by doubt, but now they stood together to enjoy the bright hopes that filled their surroundings. The vibrant array of colours that Lesedi used to paint the township became a shared narrative, a story that the entire community could relate to.

As the sun sank beneath the horizon, painting the streets with a breathtaking palette of gold and pink, Lesedi found himself lost in contemplation of the profound impact he had made. Inspired by the brilliance of dreams, these ethereal visions have left an indelible mark on the minds of the community, serving as a powerful reminder of the transformative power of art.

With a visionary gaze, He imagined a future where the vibrant tapestry of life would continue to unfurl. The walls that were once witnesses to hardships and obstacles now served as blank canvases for motivation. Lesedi noticed a familiar spark of creativity in the eyes of young artists, reminiscent of his own journey.

The radiant dreams had not only changed the walls, but had crafted a story of strength and victory. His success was a true triumph, not only for himself but for the entire community. It serves as a powerful reminder of how art has the incredible power to transcend barriers and ignite transformation.

So, He kept painting the impossible because he knew that the colours he had made would live on, not just on canvases but also in the hearts and minds of people who were brave enough to dream bigger than life. The glowing dreams had turned into a lighthouse that showed other artists how to reach the place where fantasy and reality danced together in a creative harmony.

Inspired by the brilliance of creative vision, Lesedi's dreams shone brightly, conquering the obstacles that once threatened to dim his artistic journey. Just as a tempest subsides, his passion and purpose have triumphed over the doubts and scepticism he faced.

Like a master storyteller, Lesedi had completely transformed the narrative of his existence. Every brushstroke had transformed into a powerful testament of strength, a bold rebellion against the obstacles that aimed to restrict his aspirations within the confines of uncertainty.

The streets, reminiscent of a community's past struggles, now resounded with the vibrant colours of a collective heritage. Inspired by the enchanting tales of imagination, the ethereal dreams painted on the walls spoke of profound change and the limitless possibilities that reside within the realm of artistic expression.

In His artistic journey, he encountered various challenges that tested his confidence and faced skepticism from others. However, he managed to incorporate these opposing forces into his creative process. Once doubted and challenged, the artist's self-assurance shone through his paintings, a testament to his triumph over hardship.

The town came together to see the living tapestry that had transformed their streets, and it was clear that the glowing fantasies had transformed into something more than just paintings. They embodied the triumph of many, a united voyage that went beyond personal challenges.

In the depths of the past, the defeated and subdued antagonistic forces remained in their presence a mere whisper of a forgotten time. His art had become a powerful testament to the notion that creativity, when unleashed with unwavering determination, has the ability to transform not only canvases but the very essence of reality. A new age, when art served as a symbol of inspiration and hope, was heralded by the luminous dreams, which acted as sentinels to ward against uncertainty.

The future unfurled with the vividness of a captivating tale, offering boundless inspiration and profound change for a fresh wave of artists in Sebokeng. Lesedi, with his profound artistic journey, has become a guiding light for the creative aspirations of the younger generation.

Drawn to the enchanting visions that illuminated their surroundings, the youthful individuals of the community embarked on a journey to discover the unexplored realms of their artistic abilities. Lesedi, now a mentor, discovered immense satisfaction in fostering these emerging talents, offering expert guidance akin to a seasoned sailor navigating them through the vast oceans of artistic exploration.

In the hushed corners of impromptu studios and outdoor galleries, the young artists of Sebokeng confidently painted with their brushes. People all woke up because of the glowing dreams, which turned the quiet whispers of artistic possibility into a loud choir.

Lesedi's workshop, which used to be a quiet place for her to work alone, was now full of the energy of people working together and sharing goals. The walls resounded with joyous laughter, blending harmoniously with the gentle whispers of brushes caressing canvases. In the eyes of the future artists, filled with the radiance of their dreams, Lesedi was not only a mentor but a living embodiment of the profound impact art can have.

As Lesedi imparted his wisdom and methods, the studio evolved into an intellectual gumbo, where the luminous aspirations of one creator blended in perfect harmony with those of another. The vibrant legacy of colours, started by Lesedi's adventure, kept on enchanting the community's creative tapestry.

And as the sun set, painting the sky with vibrant hues and casting enchanting shadows, Lesedi found joy in the knowledge that his art had sparked an everlasting wellspring of inspiration. His bright ideas had grown beyond the limits of his paintings and were now painting the future of Sebokeng in colours of creativity, strength, and endless possibilities.

The gallery doors swung open with a quiet grace, revealing an expanse of white walls that seemed to yearn for the touch of Lesedi's radiant visions. This invitation was not just an ordinary one; it served as a powerful reminder of the limitless potential that had emerged from his creative exploration.

As Lesedi entered the gallery, the gentle illumination of strategically placed lights danced upon the paintings adorning the walls. Every brushstroke and colour seemed to move together in perfect harmony, forming a visual masterpiece that resonated with the profound impact of artistic expression. Once just a pipe dream, the gallery is now a physical location where luminous aspirations may come to life.

Walking amidst his creations, Lesedi felt an overwhelming sense of fulfilment.

It wasn't solely about personal triumph; it was a joyous tribute to the strength portrayed in every brushstroke, a celebration of the radiant dreams that had taken root in the hearts of the community.

The streets outside, now illuminated by the gentle hues of dusk, reflected the transformation taking place within the gallery. Lesedi embraced the responsibility with a sense of honour, viewing it as a privilege rather than a burden. It wasn't only about creating stunning artworks; it was about telling a story that resonated with the shared essence of the community.

As he explored the gallery, Lesedi came to the realisation that this exhibition went beyond being just a display of art—it was a profound conversation between the artist and the community.

The radiant dreams, previously limited to the narrow streets, had now extended their influence, sharing stories of optimism and strength with all who entered the art exhibition.

At that moment, Lesedi realised that the gallery held a deeper meaning beyond being a mere space for showcasing art. It served as a powerful bridge, connecting his radiant dreams with the hopes and ambitions of those who beheld them. Inspiration was not merely a duty, but an important calling - to ignite a passionate fire within the souls of those who beheld the captivating symphony of hues upon the canvas.

Just as the final visitor departed the gallery, taking with them a fragment of the radiant dreams, Lesedi remained in the midst of his creations, a guardian of hope and a keeper of untold tales. Even though the gallery doors shut behind him, the glowing dreams kept going, going beyond the space itself and becoming a part of the legacy of colours that painted Sebokeng's creative future.

Lesedi stood at the crossroads of his life, where the threads of his past, present, and future converged. Rather than being only a reflection of the present moment, the legacy of colours, which consisted of a brilliant tapestry of glowing visions, was an eternal tale that was woven into the very fabric of the history of Sebokeng where it was located.

His murals, reminiscent of ancient manuscripts, graced the walls with timeless tales. Every brushstroke captured the essence of adversity, the victory of perseverance, and the limitless possibilities of the human soul. Not only did the gallery become a gateway to Lesedi's artistic journey, but it also served as a gateway to a series of storylines that extended far beyond the bounds of the present.

The vibrant palette, crafted by Lesedi's skilled hand, would continue to grow and transform. The murals were vibrant expressions that showcased the profound impact of art. As the sun sank beneath the horizon, painting the streets with a gentle radiance and illuminating the walls adorned with his vibrant dreams, Lesedi realised that his legacy extended far beyond the gallery and the alleys. It had become ingrained in the shared memories of Sebokeng.

The murals exuded a vibrant energy that conveyed a profound truth beyond the confines of words. They shared stories of hardship and success, perseverance and optimism, with anyone willing to truly see and hear. Lesedi, now entrusted with this rich heritage, recognised that his duty went far beyond the mere movements of his paintbrush.

In the tranquil stillness of the evening, as the vibrant hues danced in the waning light, Lesedi made a solemn promise. The murals would serve as lasting testaments to his artistic journey, illuminating the dreams and ambitions of generations to come. Inspired by the spirit of a visionary artist, the vibrant hues of Sebokeng have become a lasting testament to the power of imagination and the beauty of pushing artistic boundaries.

As Lesedi gazed at the horizon, where the radiant dreams blended with the darkness of the night, he realised that his artistic journey was more than just a personal quest—it was a collective heritage that would ignite, echo, and forever colour Sebokeng with boundless potential.

* * *

In the serene moments of the township, where the challenges of life settled like a dense mist, a remarkable change took place—a growth reminiscent of the blossoming of flowers after a refreshing spring shower. Lesedi's dreams, once soft murmurs in the halls of his mind, now flowed through narrow streets with the vivid touch of a celestial artist.

The narrow streets, once filled with doubt and uncertainty, had transformed into vibrant outdoor art exhibits. Walls that had seen the hardships of everyday existence were now adorned with tapestries of optimism. Every stroke of Lesedi's brush was a defiance against uncertainty, a declaration that imagination could conquer the darkness that lingered in the corners.

The glowing colours that now adorned the walls were captured by the sunshine as it seeped through the gaps between the humble homes. What used to be just a way to get through hard times had turned into a call for everyone to join the lively stories that were playing out on these blank canvases.

Amidst this quiet revolution, the narrow alleys ceased to tell stories of hopelessness. Instead, they resonated with the vitality of imagination, pulsating with the radiant aspirations that had surpassed the limitations of one artist's thoughts. The walls, once silent, now reverberated with tales of strength, determination, and the boldness to imagine in a world where imagination was seen as a privilege.

Passersby, who used to rush through these alleys without a second glance, now felt an irresistible urge to pause and take in the view. The radiant dreams adorning the walls were not mere reflections of Lesedi's journey; rather, they served as mirrors, revealing the aspirations of an entire community, now made visible to all.

While the gallery doors stayed locked, the lanes transformed into an open invitation. They stood as a tribute to the power of dreams, inviting everyone to see how creativity triumphed over the darkness that had previously enveloped these pathways.

Lesedi, the visionary, found himself at the intersection of the tangible and the ethereal, holding the cosmic brush as a gateway to hidden realms. Surveying the open-air galleries that were once nondescript alleyways, his heart filled with the realisation that dreams, when fuelled by passion, have the power to transcend the limits of the mind.

His spirit had become intertwined with the cosmic brush, once a source of scepticism but now a mystical enigma. Each brush-stroke served as a conduit, seamlessly merging the boundless realm of his imagination with the physical reality of Sebokeng. The radiant dreams, akin to celestial messengers, murmured stories that surpassed the limits of the mundane.

The gallery, reminiscent of the works of a renowned artist, now stood as a physical embodiment of Lesedi's odyssey. The walls were a testament to the boldness of an artist who fearlessly brought his dreams to life on the canvas. Paths that were once straightforward in life had transformed into a joyful recognition of the limitless possibilities that arise when imagination and challenges intertwine.

Lesedi, the dream-weaver, had transformed into a living embodiment of potential. The open-air galleries were vibrant showcases of art that beautifully captured the enchanting essence of vivid dreams. In the grasp of his hand, the cosmic brush became more than just a mere tool. It possessed a mystical power, transforming the ordinary into something extraordinary, the mundane into something radiant, and dreams into vivid realities.

As time went on, Lesedi's accomplishments continued to

stand out. His solo exhibition had become a yearly event that drew in art enthusiasts, critics, and those with a penchant for dreaming. Inspired by the vibrant hues that adorned the walls of the township, the community has embraced a legacy of colours that continues to inspire and fill them with pride for generations to come.

In the lively gallery, where the atmosphere buzzed with the energy of radiant dreams, Lesedi found himself surrounded by a kaleidoscope of colours that conveyed narratives beyond the realm of ordinary comprehension. Viewers were invited into a dreamscape where reality and fantasy were mixed through the use of the canvases, which were like windows to another dimension.

Every brushstroke was a graceful movement, a symphony of determination brought to life on the canvas. From simple shards of Lesedi's imagination, the glowing visions had blossomed into a symphony—a complex web of stories that lauded the resilience of the human spirit. The colours, full of life and energy, appeared to connect deeply with the emotions of those who gazed upon them.

Every single person who had entered the gallery became a part of the story as the atmosphere was filled with admiration. They meandered through the radiant dreams, their personal narratives entwined with the brushstrokes on canvas. Lesedi, the master of dreams, had not only created vivid scenes but had crafted an enchanting experience—an invitation to immerse oneself in a realm where challenges whispered stories of victory and darkness gracefully intertwined with the light.

In the gallery's lively ambiance, the radiant dreams transformed into more than mere paintings; they beckoned one to venture beyond the mundane, to discover the limitless horizons of the human imagination. Lesedi, with his artistic talent, had not only decorated walls but had created a beautiful tapestry of dreams that resonated with the shared spirit of a transformed community.

Not only had Lesedi's life been changed by the luminous dreams, but they had also become an inspiration to those who dared to dream against the odds. The young individuals, captivated by his journey, now pursued their artistic aspirations with a renewed passion. The gallery had transformed into a sanctuary where dreams were not only showcased, but also cultivated; where the canvas became a realm of infinite potential.

As the sun gracefully descended, its warm rays gently embraced the murals that graced the walls of the township. Lesedi, immersed in the enchanting embrace of twilight, stood in awe before his masterpieces. The radiant dreams, once ethereal murmurs of creativity, now throbbed with a vitality of their own.

The colours on the walls seemed to come alive with the fading light, painting stories of hardship and victory in brushstrokes that reverberated through the streets. Lesedi's artistic talent went beyond mere painting; it created a tapestry of dreams that resonated with the spirit of Sebokeng.

Lesedi felt a deep sense of contentment during the peaceful moments of the evening. As guardians of hope, the paintings showed how art has the power to change the world. Those who strolled through the township's alleyways would find live tales inscribed on the walls, transformed from luminous visions.

As Lesedi looked out at the dreamscape that enveloped the town, he couldn't help but feel a deep connection to the community, as if his story was intricately intertwined with theirs. The luminous aspirations, which had previously been contained inside his imagination, had evolved into a heritage that went beyond personal stories. They exemplified the notion that through the interplay of vibrant hues and boundless imagination, a community could discover its unique expression and shed light on the most obscure aspects of its past

In the heart of Sebokeng, where the sun caressed the walls adorned with vibrant dreams, Lesedi stood as a living testament to the profound impact of art. From a path shrouded in uncertainty, his trip had transformed into a colourful symphony that echoed through the streets and beyond.

Colours and dreams painted a story of hope that spread throughout Sebokeng.

Lesedi, a true visionary, had created a work of art that went beyond the boundaries of the canvas. The radiant dreams, etched within souls, murmured a symphony of victory amidst adversity.

As the sun set, painting the town in a warm glow, Lesedi's influence reached out to a world in need of motivation. His legacy, woven throughout the community, reminded everyone that aspirations painted with passion and effort could turn even the darkest alleyways into paths of limitless possibilities.

The radiant dreams became a language understood by all who dared to dream. Lesedi's story, captured in the vibrant murals that adorned Sebokeng, beckoned the world to embrace the enchantment of creativity. With every stroke of his brush, there resonated a profound belief that no matter what challenges one encounter, dreams can be realised, and the tapestry of existence can be adorned with the vibrant hues of boundless potential

It was a joyous occasion, where dreams were brought to life, challenges were conquered, and the profound impact of art was showcased. It conveyed a message to the readers that even in the most challenging moments of life, vivid dreams have the power to guide one toward extraordinary achievements. It served as a gentle reminder that each stroke of the universal brush held the power to craft a work of art—a work of art imbued with hope, determination, and the unwavering faith that dreams are attainable, no matter the challenges encountered.

In the realm of artistic expression, a vibrant tapestry of hues unfurled, while ethereal visions whispered their stories of inspiration to those with open hearts. And as Lesedi ventured into the night, armed with a cosmic brush, he wholeheartedly embraced the boundless expanse of the dreamscape, prepared to create fresh narratives and ignite future adventures.

Immersed in the serenity of his studio, Lesedi found himself surrounded by the vibrant tapestry of his vivid dreams. Every brushstroke became a chapter, and every hue contributed to the magnificent symphony of his artistic journey. As he traced the lines that told the story of his journey, his fingers moved with a sense of purpose, guiding the narrative like a conductor leading an orchestra. The themes that resonated through the corridors of his life were invoked with every stroke.

Hope was like a strong thread that was woven into the very structure of his paintings.

He was driven by an inner fire, a guiding light during the most uncertain times. Revisiting the earliest strokes, one can almost feel the pulse of optimism that drove him to pick up the brush, even when the world seemed draped in shadows.

Perseverance, a loyal ally, remained strong in every brush-stroke, every layer of paint that adorned the canvases of adversity. Just like an artist, the brush skilfully transformed moments of despair into strokes of determination. The trials and tribulations were transformed into a remarkable display of fortitude, a testament to the indomitable spirit that arose from confronting the tempests of uncertainty.

And there Lesedi found the enchanting ability of art, a mystical potion that elevated the ordinary to the extraordinary. His artistic journey was guided by a cosmic brush, transforming challenges into a vibrant symphony of colours. Every brush-stroke represented more than just a mere stroke on canvas; it was a testament to the transformative power of art, capable of turning ordinary moments into extraordinary stories.

As Lesedi immersed himself in the studio, enveloped by the reverberations of his own artistic odyssey, he came to the profound realisation that the story of his life, imbued with hope, resilience, and the profound impact of art, extended far beyond his individual experience. It was a powerful expression, a testament to the idea that dreams, fuelled by unwavering dedication and determination, have the ability to surpass all limits of the mind.

In the serene aftermath of the conclusion, where the final strokes of Lesedi's life had settled, there resounded a joyous commemoration. It wasn't just the end of a story; it was the buildup to the end of a song played in bright colours. The words softly spoken from the pages recounted tales of dreams turned into reality, challenges overcome, and the magical fusion of an artist and their creative prowess.

The joyous occasion wasn't an outburst of revelry, but rather a reflective recognition of the quiet struggles endured, the uncertainties overcome, and the brilliant aspirations that now adorned Lesedi's life story.

The words, akin to radiant dreams, extended beyond the pages, beckoning the readers to embrace the triumph of Lesedi. They spoke in hushed tones of a celestial artist who had not just created beautiful images but had crafted a story of strength and motivation.

The sun was setting, pouring a warm, golden light through the window of Lesedi's studio. The room was filled with the usual scent of paint and paper, and his instruments were scattered around. Lesedi sat at his desk with a sense of peace and fulfillment. He composed the final words of his deep letter, a message to people who would read and be inspired by his journey.

Lesedi grabbed up his pen as the sun fell below the horizon, casting a lovely dusk over the studio. The weight of his experiences, hardships, and victories lay on his shoulders, as did his determination to share the knowledge he had learned. This letter was his legacy, a source of hope for others who would follow in his footsteps.

Lesedi, with conviction in his eyes, wrote to those who dared to dream, "These words are for all the dreamers, artists, and those who feel like their voice is too small to be heard. I need to remind them of the greatness they possess. Remember, everyone who reads this, that creativity is the greatest energy that cannot be compared to anything else. It can heal, inspire, and bring about movement. Every brushstroke in a painting, every single note of a song, and every single word of a poem contains a bit of the soul of the person who created it. Make use of the great power that exists inside every act of creation. Do not be afraid of giving all of yourself into what you do; it is through giving yourself that we connect with others. Let your work speak your truth, for truth has the greatest power."

Love, Lesedi.

About the Author

Tebogo Khalo makes his literary debut with the release of "The Black Boy's Artistic Odyssey." Khalo, who identifies primarily as a visual artist, is presently in his last year of undergraduate study in Fine Arts at the prestigious University of the Witwatersrand.

As the youngest of two siblings, he lives with his mother, uncle, and stepfather, where he develops his creative path against a dynamic backdrop of family support and artistic discovery. Tebogo grew up in the dusty but vibrant streets of Zone 7, Sebokeng, south of Johannesburg, where he was shaped by a diverse range of social experiences.

You can connect with me on:

🌐 https://www.tebogokhalo.com

www.ingramcontent.com/pod-product-compliance
Lightning Source LLC
Chambersburg PA
CBHW010302100726
47904CB00011B/2710